Atrox
An Avalon Chronicles
Novella

Alexa Whitewolf

Atrox – An Avalon Chronicles Novella
by Alexa Whitewolf
Copyright ©2019 Alexa Whitewolf

Cover design by **Y. Nikolova at Ammonia Book Covers**

First Edition

AUTHOR'S NOTE & ACKNOWLEDGEMENTS

It's funny, when you look back on a story, to realize how it has evolved over time – in ways you never could have foreseen. Such was the case for me with *The Avalon Chronicles*. Originally meant to be only one book, it now contains three full novels and this novella, so you can imagine how none of this was according to plan.

I really, really blame Alistair/Atrox for that. From the beginning in *Avalon Dreams,* he was more than a secondary character. He was supposed to be a voiceless dog – then became a demon dog with a rather heavy dose of attitude. Then he had background story as a fallen god… One I got lost in. I wanted so desperately to display his past with Merlin that I wrote *Avalon Wishes*. And once that happened and he met Catriona, well, I just knew he would end up getting his story.

This novella is meant to wrap up the series, but I can't promise you won't see Atrox in another future series of mine. He's just that lovable, once you get over his arrogance ☺

A huge thank you as always to my husband, my mom and my furbabies for helping out with the book!

To the team behind it – you guys rock! Huge extra thanks to Candace Robinson for being my trustworthy beta!!! And a master thanks to Y. Nikolova for the cover!!

To all my readers – this one's for you!

Happy readings,
Alexa

"Love is the source of every virtue in you and of every deed which deserves punishment."
- Dante Alighieri -

PROLOGUE

Atrox looked behind at his protégée one more time. For eons and lifetimes, he had protected the Lady of the Lake, most recently in this new life. She had reincarnated into Vivienne to a modern existence in Avignon, France. The forces of darkness – in the shape of the sorcerer Carleigh – had once again tried to kill her one chance at true happiness. It had been a long, hard journey to reinstate her memories and help save her soulmate's – Sébastien's – soul, but they had made it through.

Now she stood across a lake, glowing with an inner light, despite the tears streaking her cheeks. Parting ways was always hard, but he drew comfort in the life he left her to.

Vivienne's green eyes no longer held the hint of darkness. Sébastien was by her side, his arm around her waist, palm splayed in an unconsciously protective gesture over her womb – and the life building within.

A child....

As though hearing his awed thought, her features softened in understanding, and her smile became encouraging. "Safe travels, Atrox."

Their eyes met and held for a long moment, centuries of friendship passing between them. It was not truly a goodbye – only a temporary departure. At least, that was what Atrox tried to tell himself when he turned his back on the couple and dove into the water headfirst.

He emerged a few feet farther, almost near the vortex Vivienne and Sébastien had helped him to open, and glanced back. *Until we meet again.*

Atrox turned away, smiling to himself. Vivienne had grown from the child he had once met as a demon dog, to the woman he had protected through many lifetimes. And now she was secure in her identity as the Lady of the Lake, her memories no longer foggy, but all her own.

Their enemies were gone, including Morgana and Mordred – though where the sorceress had gone to, Atrox could only guess.

So it was with a clear conscience he sensed the tug of magic, of the channel taking him where he needed to be, and surrendered to it. He had something else to do, a deeper calling tugging at him.

His existence had always been lonely, but one particular spitfire had burned through it like a comet. It had been thanks to her that he had found himself, regained his powers, and managed to help Vivienne. Their relationship had been a tryst of tangled limbs and long nights, of dreams and wishes, but now he wanted the real thing.

The only problem was, Catriona was nowhere to be found. She had disappeared after her kingdom had been ruined by their enemy, Carleigh. The last time he'd seen her flashed through his mind, as did her beautiful blue eyes, filled with pain.

Atrox had only one choice – to go after her wherever she was, even if that meant landing in her father's kingdom. Only Merlyddus was not just a Fae, but the most powerful of them all. Given his kin and Atrox's had been at war, and Faes alone were capable to kill gods – and vice versa – Atrox was not fond of the idea.

But he had to try. Nothing else would suffice, nothing else would let him rest in peace. He needed Catriona by his side.

Will the Faes allow me entrance, even?

The thought was nagging, but he pushed it aside. Instead, Atrox focused his mind on flaming hair and cerulean-blue eyes. The body of a goddess. The spirit of a nymph.

Catriona.

Atrox closed his eyes, and surrendered to the water that pulled him under. He needed to see her, to explain his hesitation – his fear. He was not proud of it, but the human sentiment had gotten the best of his wary soul.

Like a tornado, images assailed him, of his time as Alistair.

The first time he'd seen Catriona.

In a parallel realm, Alistair was back in deity form, glaring at the same door he had been staring at for what felt like ages.

He sensed a shift behind and turned to see a figure step out of the darkness. She had wavy red hair, startling blue eyes and a petite figure. What most surprised him were the two wings protruding from her back, thin and shiny like a butterfly's. Only the tips were visible from where he stood, and only under a certain light.

"What now?" Alistair half-groaned mockingly. "So

this entire time, I have been kept at bay from my peaceful slumber by Faes?"

The woman laughed – tinkling bells – before settling an amused gaze on him. "Nay, wolf. It is your own kin that keep you away."

The first time he'd kissed her.

"If I am such a child," Catriona whispered seductively, "then why is your body so eager to claim me?"

"Get out of my head!" Alistair ordered, towering over her.

Catriona threw her head back, but kept her eyes locked onto his defiantly. "I was not in your head, wolf. Your body is doing all the talking."

Alistair's nostrils flared in anger, even as they squared off. Then, before he could tell himself it was a bad idea, his arms snaked around her waist and pulled the Fae closer.

His mouth descended on Catriona's brutally, even as her body pressed against his. She reached both arms around his neck, wrapping them tightly. For the first time in eons, Alistair felt a lick of desire, a flame of passion burning within.

The first time he'd claimed her...

"Why refuse yourself the delight?" Catriona smirked. "Are you afraid...Atrox?"

"I no longer go by that name," Alistair scowled.

"Perhaps not... But your wolf does."

Catriona touched his chest with one hand and the tiny flicker inside him that desired her burst into a flame, scorching through.

Alistair pulled the Fae closer, dropping his mouth to hers. At the back of his mind, the demon tried to push past the haze of desire, but it was to no avail. Catriona's body felt too good against his.

The last time he'd seen her...

"Catriona, wait!" he shouted, no longer caring of the desperation that tinged his voice.

"Please, I–" He stopped, the words locked in his throat.

And his own admission, not so long ago, to Sébastien.

"What happened?"

"She had to leave."

Sébastien frowned, unsure he had heard correctly. "Leave? As in for a short time or...?" Alistair's silence provided the answer once more, and he knew no words of consolation would help.

After a beat, it was the wolf god who spoke. "I had a choice to keep her, to admit my feelings. Perhaps it would have changed things, perhaps not. But I did not take it, and instead I let her walk away."

"Why?"

"Carleigh followed her in her realm, and they fought until she chased him out. When I last saw it, her entire kingdom had been destroyed."

All the scenes of the past crossed his mind as the vortex took him. Since Catriona had left him, he'd done nothing but mope around. Highly undignified for one who had regained his deity abilities, and had been part of a pantheon of gods.

The problem was that Catriona wasn't only in his head. She was in his heart, in his soul. And worst of all, he liked it that way. Her walking out of his life did, in no shape or form, fulfill that craving.

And one way or another, Atrox planned to get her back.

Make her see they belonged together.

And if I have to go to the gates of Hell itself, then so be it.

≈ ♠ ≈

The nauseating spinning finally came to an end, and the water pushed him towards a surface. As a past god, part of a pantheon of rulers, he was well in tune with the ways of travelling. More than once, he had used his sister's – Ardea's – tunnels to enter Earth. However, not even those trips could account for the morbid nausea he suffered through on his current journey.

It must be the Fae's doing – to keep others away.

Atrox was pushed further up, up – his ears popped – and then out into a vividly blue sky. His body flew through the air and landed in a crouch on the closest piece of land.

Even as he panted, trying to regain his breath, Atrox knew he was in trouble. Rather than a clearing similar to the one he was used to in Catriona's realm, he found himself surrounded by Faes – males. In armor. With spears.

"Shite!" he cursed under his breath.

He *had* thought of Catriona, though, so why would Vivienne's spell bring him here? The cynical part of him quickly pointed out she had crossed him, but he knew that was untrue the moment the thought formed. *More than likely it's that I was right all along, and Catriona must be here, in this place...* Now if only he could get past those who opposed him.

Still in a crouch, he took stock of his opponents. Ten, twenty? Some were tall like him, their Fae wings displayed in a distinctively offensive attack, so he couldn't see if others hid behind them.

But the vivid colours of the sky, the smell in the air – they were unmistakable. *I'm definitely not on any earthly realm.*

Above all others, Atrox thought he could smell Catriona's unique scent. It was faint, but the flowery tones were definitely presently in the air. Enough with the foolishness, he chastised himself. *These Faes look ready to gut me. Time to try out my newly regained powers.*

Just as he started gathering the divine energy at his disposal, someone spoke, making the air itself vibrate.

"I thought I was clear when we last saw each other, mongrel."

The wolf god whirled around, his midnight gaze falling on Merlyddus. He had only seen Catriona's father once, but it had been enough. That encounter flashed through his mind, and he gritted his teeth at the reminder.

The man inclined his head, but made no comment once more, leaving Alistair free to proceed. "Then you are aware they left Merlin behind. It so happens Carleigh also dropped a magical gadget there. It is set to explode around the same time Vivienne will be sacrificed, killing Merlin as well."

For a long moment, Merlyddus said nothing. When he spoke again, the hard tone was not what Alistair had expected.

"Keep your nose out of this, wolf god. I can protect my son, but I warn you for the last time to stay the hell away from them going forward. Are we understood?"

His dark gaze settled on Merlyddus, noticing some of the same rigidity in his posture. Seated on his throne, the elder Fae was holding onto a cane much like another's. *I guess it's a familial trait, Merlin.*

Atrox pushed aside thoughts of the half-Fae mage he'd

helped through the ages, focusing instead on his father. The old man's glare was icy. "You were warned to stay out of my business."

Rather than cower, the wolf god rose to his full height, onyx eyes flashing with a red light. "I heard you loud and clear, Fae king." A gaze around, then he spoke just as ominously. "But I did not come here for you. I've come to take home what is mine."

The king's eyes glittered menacingly, but still he asked, "And what would that be?"

Atrox smirked. "Catriona."

CHAPTER 1

A moment of stupefaction zinged around, then Merlyddus laughed. It started off as a chuckle, then slowly turned into a full, booming guffaw. Some of the Fae guards joined him, but the rest maintained their stoic expressions, massive spears in hand.

Atrox only scowled, resisting the urge to blast his way through Catriona's kinsmen. If she really was there, he needed to be cool, collected, and express his feelings in a way that was —

"Are you done yet, yeah?"

Merlyddus stopped laughing abruptly at his rude tone. Those blue eyes – so fucking similar to Merlin's – settled on him in much the same way his former friend's had.

"What makes you think Catriona would go with you anywhere, for that matter?"

Bite your tongue. Bite your ton—

"You mean, besides the fact we've shagged more than once, and I'm pretty damn sure she's in love with me?"

Not even his rational mind had been able to keep him from putting his foot in his mouth. Atrox refused to back down, though. Instead, he lifted his chin up and returned Merlyddus' glare with one of his own. "I want your daughter by my side, for all the eons to come. So wherever she is in this blasted realm, send out a party – or whatever it is you do – and bring her here." A beat later, he added, "If you would so kindly."

A rumble of dissatisfaction rang through the soldiers. And was it his imagination, or were those spears getting closer? A trickle of unease spread through him.

Long ago, Faes and gods had fought, with losses on both sides. The Long Wars had only ended because both races had deigned to put their pride aside, and realize losing so many of their own kind was not serving any one's purposes. Strict rules had been put into place to separate Faes from gods, with the former living in separate realms, and the latter in pantheons only accessible to the divine.

Or, so they thought.

Atrox knew first hand that Faes could access the gods pantheon, even their ever after realm, and deities were none the wiser. After all, had it not been how Catriona had helped him, following his death in the past?

He recalled her words as clearly as if she whispered them in his ear. *You are the rule followers, and we are the breakers.*

Atrox clenched one fist, feeling his own newly retrieved power at the ready. He was about to break the dictates of his pantheon, and engage with Faes. Perhaps it was not what he was supposed to do with his second chance at divine immortality, but he was not about to stand down.

I'll fight through them if I must, but I'd really rather not leave a trail of corpses behind on my way to you, Catriona.

Nothing answered his mental call – he hadn't really counted on it, either. After all, Catriona had been quiet ever since she'd left him. But what if it wasn't of her own volition?

Atrox's eyes narrowed on the king, whose own expression matched his, in stone. "I don't see you sending your scouts for her. So either you're planning to fight me – which would be a bad idea – or you have no plans to bring Catriona here. For your sake, I'm hoping it's the first."

"And if it is not?" Merlyddus asked, anger vibrating in his voice.

"Then that would imply you're holding her captive, which would make me very, very angry." Both fists clenched, he spread his feet for better balance. Something rippling in the air warned he was close – nay, *they* were close – to exploding.

Merlyddus gave one nod – that was all they needed. The Fae warriors around him moved in, tightening the circle, their spears aimed for him. Their mistake was moving as if they had all the time in the world.

Everyone knows that to catch a wolf, you need to move like one.

Snorting, Atrox clenched his other fist. A silver blaze escaped his palms, travelling over his human form, until it left him as a wolf. The spears were suddenly no longer pointed at his heart, but rather in midair over his head.

Eyes glowing red, jaws snarling, Atrox lunged at the Fae closest to him and yanked the spear out of his befuddled hands. In a spur of quickness, he did the same to the entire circle, then resumed his human form. Hands up in a boxing stance, he smirked at the captain of the guard.

"I'm all yours, pretty boy."

Blue eyes – what was it with all the Faes and their damn blue eyes – flashed at him, and the man stepped forward. Only, they were obviously not warriors trained in hand-to-hand combat. One smack to his nose via the palm of his hand, and the steel helmet broke it. Blood gushed out, tainting the ground around them.

"You dare draw blood, on this sacred ground?" Merlyddus' rage seemed to have increased.

Out of the corner of his eye, Atrox noticed the old man get up from the throne he'd been occupying. His brows were tightly drawn together, and the crystal atop his staff glowed. Air was electrified, as were the Faes, and Atrox recalled with clarity exactly how much emotions influenced a Fae's powers.

Judging by the looks of this, I've really managed to piss him off.

"You, a childish divinity, less than half my age, think you can come here and trample over all I have built?" Merlyddus stood straighter, and the staff pointed straight at Atrox's chest. "I think not. Seize him."

Did he not just see me wipe out his guards?

Atrox's confusion gave way to incredulity when he tried to move – and realized he could not. Whatever Merlyddus was doing, it was interfering with his own power. Though Atrox had only vague knowledge of Fae magic, he could sense the energy wrapping around him, immobilizing him. Rather than let it go, he yanked on it. The old king's eyes shone with that unnatural edge Catriona always had in hers.

Then something hit Atrox over the back of his head, and he swayed. Another smack, and this time he dropped to one knee. Blood pooled around him. A third hit, and his second knee met the ground, along with his palms.

Faes played dirty in the war, he recalled his brother, Aequus, tell him once. Well, now he knew what that meant.

Blinking, struggling to hold on to consciousness, he lifted his head. Merlyddus was now in front of him, looking down at him. "Do what you will, old man. I will have Catriona, come what may."

It was the oddest thing. Merlyddus' features contorted in rage – for the briefest of moments. Then he was, once more, the solemn old man. "You must be deluded if you believe Catriona has feelings for you, wolf god. She is much smarter than that."

The staff was pointed at him again, and he collapsed on the softest grass, tinged with his blood.

≈ ♠ ≈

The footsteps woke him first, and Atrox jerked to a crouch. In the pitch darkness of the tower, he could see the shapes of those imprisoned by the king. Faes who had done wrong, and were awaiting their punishment in obscurity, deprived of the light they all needed. Even they did not speak to him – he was a different being, an Other. He was a divinity.

And here? He was a pariah.

"Damn wars of long past," he grumbled, standing and cracking his neck. "As if I have time to waste."

Merlyddus might have used his elemental strength to put him down, but his own divine powers had healed him in his sleep. A touch at the back of his head confirmed what had been cracked open was now sealed, with a thin patch of hair grown back over it.

Atrox scowled at the shadows. He was out of his league,

surrounded by Faes who could – and would – hurt him with a single order from the king. And he was nowhere close to tracking Catriona, not if she was cloaked by her father's powers.

The old king hated Atrox, had ever since he had known they were fooling around. By all accounts, him and Catriona were not meant to be. Yet the beating of his heart when he thought of her, the aching in his chest since she'd left, told him something completely different.

It's about damn time I get out of here and find her.

On steady footsteps, he marched to the silvery bars holding him captive. With clenched fists, he hit them, making the hinges rattle. His strength was enough to make the entire dungeon tremble, and the imprisoned Faes cowered in fear.

"Oy! Get the king, will you? I need a word with him."

One of the guards stepped closer, his angelic features twisted in a smirk. He'd been watching Atrox ever since he'd stirred. "And who do you think you are, giving orders here?"

Atrox looked him from head to toe, and echoed the smirk. "Way above your station, fool. Bring me to Merlyddus and stop wasting my time."

The Fae narrowed his eyes, and jabbed the point of his spear through the bars. He narrowly missed Atrox when he shifted out of the way. "You think yourself worthy of Catriona? Perhaps *you* are the fool, after all."

Atrox snarled and grabbed the point of the spear before the guard could remove it. "It's your prerogative to think so. But we both know I'm better suited than you for Catriona. That's why you're being an asshole, isn't it? You wanted her?"

The guard scowled. "Shut your mouth."

Atrox let go of the spear and took a step back, opening

his arms. "Come get me, then. You know you want to."

The Fae's face contorted further, and just as he'd predicted, his baser impulses took over. He jerked the jail door and stepped inside. The spear was thrown to the floor, instead replaced by a sword glinting in the dark.

Atrox tried to hold back a smile. He failed.

The guard did not see him coming. One minute, he was standing and waiting for the blow. The next, Atrox dropped to the ground while kicking at the Fae's feet, and grabbed the weapon out of his hand effortlessly. With a sweeping gesture, he got back to his feet, this time with the guard in a headlock and the sword at his throat.

The Fae was panting against his iron hold, but Atrox merely smiled coldly. "You seem to have misunderstood me. It was not a request, Fae. Take me to see the king. *Now*."

The guard had no choice. Little by little, he led Atrox to the throne room. The two Faes guarding the entrance took out their weapons, but Atrox shook his head once. "I'd think twice about that, if I was you."

The sword at their kinsman's throat was enough to convince them to listen. Step by step, they walked across a narrow hallway, then turned a corner and crossed through large, oak doors.

When he followed inside, Atrox made sure to keep an eye on the Faes at his back.

"What is the meaning of this?"

He glanced at Merlyddus and his entourage, surrounding yet another throne, this one carved out of oak as aged as the doors. "Thought it was time we spoke properly, since you so rudely sent me to the dungeons before."

Merlyddus arched an eyebrow, his icy gaze glaring at Atrox. "You dare defy me in my own realm?"

The wolf god glanced around. "Colourful realm, yes. As I said, I've come here for Catriona. Where is she?"

Merlyddus stood from his throne, his glare intensifying. Atrox had seen the same look on Merlin, and threw the guard towards the king just as he tried to charm the elements his way.

The attack fizzed out like fireworks without a fuse, and Atrox grinned. "Won't harm one of your own, will you? I know your tricks, old man. You forget I met your son."

Merlyddus stopped in his movements, squinting at him. Then he waved his hand towards the entourage, which had been stealthily trying to get nearer Atrox. "Leave us."

They stared at him incredulously, and that alone inflated Atrox's ego. *They're scared of me. Good.*

Once they were left alone, Merlyddus pointed to a cushion by the stairs of the throne. "Take a seat. Eat." He then gestured to a nearby table filled with vibrant fruits, each more exotic-looking than the next.

Atrox scoffed. "Don't think so. Where is Catriona?"

Rather than answer, the old king took some grapes and started eating them one by one. With each crunch of his teeth, Atrox felt his control slipping.

The old man liked playing games, that much he knew. He was also very good at coming between him and Catriona, not that he intended to let him do so again.

When his fists clenched again, Atrox growled, "Highness, if you please.... I know we have eternity, but I really need to see your daughter."

"Why? You broke her heart."

His nonchalant response gave Atrox pause. "You...know?"

Merlyddus threw him an amused glance. "I know everything."

Atrox narrowed his eyes. "Meaning you've seen her. She *is* here." The certainty filled his blood, but also fuelled his rage. "Why all these games, Merlyddus?"

Another grape popped into his mouth, the juice dripping down his chin and into his beard. With unhurried movements, Merlyddus grabbed a napkin and dabbed at himself, until all traces of the offending juice had been removed.

Each movement was designed to drive Atrox out of his mind. He knew it. Of course the king would play games – riddles. But did he have to be so...damn....slow?

Atrox took a step closer, gritting his teeth. "I asked you a question."

"Mm, more than one, as I recall."

Still that even tone, unhurried, ready to make him snap. Atrox focused on his breathing, refusing to give in – yet so close to losing it. "You don't plan to tell me."

A flicker of a smile was his answer.

"Fine, then. I'll find her myself."

Atrox turned on his heels and stomped towards the door, but found it locked. He threw his divine magic at it, to no avail. "Enough with the games, old fool! Either let me out, or answer my damn questions."

"I do not think so," Merlyddus said in a deadly whisper.

When Atrox turned to face him, he had the king's full attention, his staff in hand and ready for a duel by the looks of it. "You have entered this realm without my permission, and I fully intend to ensure you will not leave – unless I so wish it."

"If you keep me here, I will make sure to rain hell on this beautiful piece of heaven. I used to be lord of that particular underworld, don't you know?"

Merlyddus' eyes twinkled. "A formidable foe, I see. And yet, you are still only a divinity."

Atrox gritted his teeth at the insult, and stepped closer still. "Fine, old man. So what is it you wish?"

Merlyddus stared at the plate of fruits as if it alone held all the secrets. In the end, he settled for a piece of something that looked like purple pineapple. "I have a better question," he said. "What would you do for Catriona?"

"What?"

The king turned to him, plopping the fruit in his mouth. "To what extent would you go, for a chance to see her again?"

"See her, or leave with her?"

Merlyddus' eyes widened in mock innocence. "Whatever do you mean?"

"Stop taking me for a fool!" Atrox took a deep breath, then lowered his voice. "I've had it with your duplicitous nature and spoken riddles. I know it was you who told her about Merlin's dilemma – and what I hid, to spare her pain. All to drive a wedge between us. It was the last thing she told me, and probably contributed to her leaving me."

The Fae chewed thoughtfully, then shrugged in a much too graceful gesture. "If she left you, what are you doing here, then? I know my daughter. She must have made herself very, very clear. Is her rejection not enough once? You wish for more?"

"Play your mind games with someone else."Atrox

refused to let doubt get to him, but he also found it hard to leave without answers. *I didn't get my powers and identity back for nothing.* Out loud, he said, "What guarantees me whatever this is, would end with me leaving this realm – with her?"

Merlyddus grinned, but said nothing. Atrox narrowed his eyes. Either he walked out, forced his way out, all without knowing where Catriona was. Or, he played to the old fool's tune, until it got him what he wanted.

The choice, in the end, was easy. He sighed, affecting a contrite air. "Very well. The answer is I'd do anything for Catriona, no doubt about it."

The Fae king's grin turned positively radiant as he clapped. "Wonderful! And this includes humouring an old man and his games, I suppose?"

Fucking hell, but he's bonkers. Shaking his head, Atrox nodded. "Yeah. I said anything, didn't I?"

"Indeed, you did." Something about his tone made the wolf god aware of just who, exactly, Merlin got his trickery and manipulative side from.

Merlyddus walked a few steps away from the fruits, and with one sweep of his hand, and one of his staff, he opened a portal. It shimmered like water between worlds, though all Atrox could see on the other side was darkness.

Something clenched in the pit of his stomach. It wasn't fear – but an odd sensation, like an instinct warning him against going wherever that door led.

"You have two choices, wolf. Step through this and be faced with seven challenges. Make no mistake, they will not be easy. But if you survive them all, you can see Catriona."

"So she *is* here." It was his last attempt at confirming

her presence, but Merlyddus only grinned, his expression unreadable. Atrox sighed, pinching the bridge of his nose. "And if I do not survive?"

One shoulder of the king's lifted in a careless shrug. "You die in the challenge, and lose her. Or, you can walk away now and forget about her."

Despite his nonchalant attitude, his eyes betrayed him. There was a hint of something in there – a dare. And Atrox was not one to live down such a dare. However, the stakes were not clear, and he had no idea what he was stepping into.

Last time he'd died, he had spent a rather ungodly amount of time waiting at the gates of heaven for deities. Would that be the case this time? Did he even have another life left?

Atrox glanced at the portal, weighing the options. There really weren't any, if he wanted Catriona.

"Do you hesitate, wolf?"

He glared at the old king. "Not for value of my life, but because of Catriona. Is she safe? Answer me that, at least." Like sand passing through his lips, he added the one word he had never said. "Please."

Merlyddus' glare pinned his. "Yes."

Atrox nodded, relief spreading through him. Rolling one shoulder, then the next, he faced the portal. "Then tell Catriona I will see her on the other side."

Without a backwards glance, he stepped through the portal, and into the beyond.

CHAPTER 2

Atrox rolled to avoid a hit and ended in a crouch, nearly kissing the ground. Dust surrounded him and as he coughed, and it took a moment for his eyes to adjust. When they did, he frowned.

A dark hallway stretched ahead of him, leading to who knew where. He glanced behind himself, but there was no trace left of the portal that had brought him there. Something slithered in the shadows and he turned to the noise, but could see nothing past it.

Lifting a hand, he called forth some of his divine energy, enough to cast a glow around the edges of what he had landed in. The ground was grimy, not quite sandy, but not a regular road like the humans'.

I'm neither in Fae, nor human territory, then, he mused.

Another slithering caused him to narrow his eyes further, and then he rolled his shoulders, and stepped forth. There was no point in standing and staring, when Merlyddus had been clear. He had a task – or seven – awaiting, which meant in order to do the challenges, he needed to first encounter them.

Minutes turned into hours as Atrox walked, though it did not feel like he was actually moving forward. More overwhelming was the sensation of being watched, and being someone else's pawn.

Merlyddus must be enjoying it.

Atrox knew the old king had probably sent him on a wild goose chase, but he had not been about to back down from a dare. Unfortunately, unless he was willing to portal himself out of there, he was out of luck.

Then again, he mused, it had been a while since someone challenged him quite to this level. Watching over Vivienne, helping her in her quest to fight Carleigh, had been his job for the last centuries. Yet with his abilities limited until recently, he had never been able to play the role he wanted.

Now that he was back to his regular wolf god self, he should have craved his power of old. The machinations, the manipulations… Yet he found himself not wanting it, but rather yearning for Catriona. *Odd, indeed.*

Atrox slowed his steps as he arrived at an entrance. From afar, it seemed like a cavern, but there was nothing natural about it. He waited until he was closer to have a better look, but there was no mistaking the distinct overwhelming scent coming off it.

The entrance he was in was familiar, a little too much so...

"That shite king," he muttered.

Yes, it was indeed familiar. Eons ago, it had been his kingdom. His underworld to protect, to rule, until he had been kicked out for helping Merlin.

"So that's his plan, to send me fighting my old

demons?" Atrox snorted. "The old fool should've thought better. This and more, I'll do for Catriona."

He held one hand in front of him, and a jet of flames left it. A sword materialized in his grip, its blade glinting softly. *Like my brother always said, one should not be stupid enough to bring fists alone to a fight.*

Weapon in hand, he crossed the threshold into the underworld, ready to be welcomed by old friends – Darkness itself.

Atrox had one foot in the shadows and was ready to take another step when the air changed, causing him to glance behind. A woman stood facing him, her long, raven hair tied off at the back. She had one eye green as the emeralds, the other black like the night. Her features showed a wisdom past the age portrayed, and she wore a robe with a hawk brooch on one shoulder.

Tension ran through him at the sight, and he pulled back from the entrance, though he stopped a few feet away from her. "Ardea," he called.

"Brother." Her eyes flickered to the entrance behind him, and she took a step closer. "What are you doing back here?"

"The better question is, what are you?"

Ardea shook her head. "We felt... I could not let you go in, without warning you. The old Fae king has more than monsters planned for you."

"And you think I don't know this?"

She sighed, tried to reach for his hand, but he pulled away from her touch. "Why do this, then?"

"You would not understand, sister, and every moment

spent with you is another away from her." Turning on his heels, he stepped back across the entrance. Still, Ardea called out to him.

"You have changed, from the old lord of the underworld. Do not expect the darkness to welcome you with open arms."

"It never did," Atrox muttered over a shoulder, then disappeared within.

≈ ♠ ≈

As he stomped his way inside what used to be his home, Atrox grumbled under his breath. It was so like Ardea to have shown up, all judgemental and delivering cryptic warnings. She had screwed up one too many things for him in the past to pay attention to, but he tried to let that go in order to focus on his quest.

Or whatever the hell this is.

The entrance gave way to another hallway, though this one looked as though it had been carved into the mountain itself. Atrox hesitated for a step, eyes narrowed on the shape of things. Much had changed since his eons there, and not for the first time he wondered who, exactly, had taken over since he had left.

Then he shook the thought from his head, and further moved in. With each step, the air became less oppressive, and more like a comfortable blanket that welcomed him home. It would be easy, so easy, to forget himself and take back what had once been his.

You have returned...

Yes...

Stay with us...

The darkness was speaking to him, as it had long ago.

Atrox forced his ears to remain oblivious, but it was not as easy to ignore the whispers now that he was no longer the one controlling it.

"Enough!" he shouted at the shadows around him, only faintly brightened by the glow of his sword. "I am here for one purpose, and one alone: to get through the seven trials and see Catriona."

Silence answered him, and he thought that was the end of it. Yet within moments, the whispers started again, this time more convincing.

Seven trials of fire and hell…

Why try, when you can own it all?

Stay with us, stay with us…

Take back what is still yours…

Atrox stopped dead in his tracks, the hairs on the back of his neck alerting him that he was being watched. *Merlyddus, again.*

Yet it was not the old Fae king who showed up in front of him. Rather, darkness itself formed a shape – a woman. It must have gone in his mind, modelling itself after his memories, for she had wavy hair down to her waist, and wings protruding from her back. But the hair was dark, the complexion ash, nothing like Catriona's flaming curls and tanned skin.

Still, the creature moved towards him, lifting a hand in greeting and smiling. *Stay with me…*

Atrox lifted the sword, pointing its tip to her neck. "Perhaps I wasn't clear enough – I am not interested."

The lifeless eyes glinted, as though not used to rejection. He knew that was the case, having been the lord of the place. Such knowledge did not escape him just because he was no longer in charge.

"Now tell me who I need to see, and what I have to do, to get the first trial out of the way. Or else, let me be."

The creature floated in midair, watching him with malice, then turned to the side and pointed in the distance. The way forward she showed was as foggy as before, and Atrox scowled.

"Thanks for nothing."

Ignoring her, he headed onwards, but was ready to whirl around and cut through her form at a moment's notice. It was not needed, however, as Darkness went back to the shadows, and he moved further inside.

Or so he thought.

A moment later, another shape burst through. Atrox lifted the sword to defend himself, and though it slashed at the creature, he also sensed something touching his shoulder.

He moved out of the way, but not fast enough. By the time he glanced to his shoulder, he noticed a mark like a hand there, darkening against his olive skin. An odd sensation, like a burn, spread through the skin, then vanished.

"What the hell did you do to me?"

Marked you, as ours…

Three days you have for your challenges…

Otherwise, you stay here…

Ours, forever more.

Atrox scowled and looked upwards, though he knew he was alone. "Are you going to do anything about this, Fae king? We had a fucking deal!"

Nothing answered him, and Atrox snorted. "Didn't think so."

Watching his back this time, he kept walking. So darkness had marked him – none of that reduced his will to move forward. *I'll simply have to run through all seven challenges faster.*

With that in mind, Atrox quickened his step. Moments later, he finally emerged out of the long tunnel into a larger cavernous space. And in its middle were the ruins of the palace he had once inhabited.

As lord of the underworld, he had turned it into a hospitable place, much like what he had been used to in his own pantheon. A palace had been a must, a luxury he had permitted himself. Seeing it in ruins brought back memories of his eons there.

"You dare step back in here?"

Atrox stopped in his tracks, and tilted his head to the side. "Who speaks?"

A cackle like a hyena's sounded. He narrowed his eyes on the darkness. "Too coward to face me?"

A different voice said, "Coward? Yes...that was always your impression of me, was it not?"

Out of the shadows, a monster stepped out. It had the body of a massive bear, only its head was split into two. One side had a mop of red hair, while the other was fully blonde. Atrox's expression cleared with stunning. "Vulper! Faitus?"

Long ago, the redheaded fox god had been his enemy, until Atrox had killed him, snuffing out his existence. Faitus had been an accomplice in Atrox's rebellion, and thrown into the underworld for his efforts. Both had died, more or less at his hands.

The heads cackled, the sound raking on Atrox's nerves.

"I thought I killed you, once."

"And so you did," Vulper said.

"You only forgot all about me," Faitus added.

Atrox narrowed his eyes. Seeing his old nemesis alive – of sorts – was not something he had been prepared to do. What was Merlyddus playing at, exactly? And why did it feel like this creature had taken his place in the underworld? Worse still, why did he care?

More cackles echoed, and Atrox shook off his thoughts. Then he lifted his hand. "No matter. I assume I'm here to fight you?" He snorted, and grasped the hilt of his sword with both hands, swishing it in the air. The mark on his arm throbbed as if to let him know he was on a timer. "So, let us get to it."

≈ ♠ ≈

It can't be a coincidence Merlyddus' first challenge brings my past to light.

Atrox jumped out of the creature's way, and slashed at a paw – missing it, but only just. The bear barrelled through the short distance and Atrox jumped in the air, avoiding him again.

He lifted a palm and called on to his divine energy, hoping to blast him and be done with it – but nothing happened. His mark throbbed, and Atrox scowled. *Did the darkness also block my powers?*

"Thought this would be easy?" Vulper taunted. Its two heads tilted in sync to the side, and something akin to a grin tugged at the lips of both beasts. "No magic allowed, wolf god. Only hand to hand combat." He lifted a paw, showing the claws. "Or rather, hand to paw."

Atrox ducked the next attack and swung the sword, hitting something – but Vulper only moved away, not giving an inkling to being hurt.

As he paced to the other side, eyes intent on not missing an attack, Atrox thought back to his past life.

When he'd been cast out of the pantheon to the underworld, one deity had taken his place among the trinity – Vulper. The god had been cunning, manipulative, and a master at winning. He had also been the cause for Atrox losing something very precious to him – Deasa.

As punishment for his wrong doings, Atrox found Vulper later, and broke the Cardinal Rule of the gods – he took another deity's life. It was an offence punishable by his own death, but no one had found out. Namely, because he had killed Vulper in between realms, and Merlin's Fae magic had created a loophole for him. As well, since the Rule demanded he pay with a life, Atrox had done so – by shedding his own identity, and taking on another. He'd become Alistair, Vivienne's guardian, and left the mess of his godly life behind.

Until recently. It had been Catriona who had helped him get it all back, little by little.

I wonder what other ghosts from my past will come to haunt me next, he thought.

Before he could think more on it, Vulper lunged. Atrox ran towards him, ducking under his large bulk and managing to scrape the sword on his underbelly, and slash at one of his back paws.

But the cut had been superficial, and though Vulper was now bleeding, the injury did not seem to bother him. "You think I will let you vanquish me again?" A cold laughter escaped him. "Nay, not today." The eyes glowed red. "Not ever again."

When he lunged, Atrox didn't get out of the way in time.

Vulper's paws rattled his chest and he tumbled to the ground, the massive beast atop him. Atrox felt its claws dig in, and Faitus' face appeared next to Vulper's. "Who's the weakling coward now?"

Atrox bared his teeth. Faitus struck with his head, biting his shoulder and holding on to it. Atrox could feel the teeth sink into his skin, ripping the muscle underneath, crunching the bone.

An agonized shout escaped him at the pain, even as he struggled to move out of the way. Vulper cackled above him. "This was much too easy."

"Not...quite."

Remembering what he'd said about hand to paw, Atrox gritted his teeth against the pain, refusing to let it take him under. *Vulper is not the only one with a primitive side.* Rather than bow in submission, Atrox reached out with both arms, wrapping his fists around Vulper's front paws. Pulling on his full abilities, he pushed against the weight, and little by little, it forced the creature to shift.

Atrox tossed him off in one last effort, then rolled to his knees, panting.

"How can this be possible?"

"You said he didn't have his full powers anymore!" Faitus whined.

Atrox lifted his head, blood seeping from his chest and shoulder, and grinned. "Surprise." He then picked up the sword in his non-mangled arm, tightened his grip around the hilt, and strode towards the creature.

He saw death in Faitus' eyes, and it numbed the pain even more.

≈ ♠ ≈

The last head rolled to the ground, and Atrox spit out blood. He held onto his bleeding shoulder. First the mark, now he was bleeding – and heavily so.

Unused to feeling so weak, he leaned against the ruins, and allowed himself to drop to the ground. The sword was still in his hand, and he refused to release it. Yet his eyelids were growing heavier, his breathing more laboured.

There was something he had to do... A healing... His wounds... Words jumbled in his mind, and he closed his eyes, letting sleep overcome him.

"What are you doing, lover?"

Her voice.

Atrox was still in the ruins area, but the entire place had a halo around it, as though it was not real. He looked around, desperately trying to find the source of the voice, and almost stopped breathing when he saw her.

Catriona was a few meters away, bathed in light. "Catriona!"

Red, flaming hair curled around her shoulders. Her blue eyes shone of an unnatural – yet distant – light. And though her body was enrobed in a beautiful purple shawl, as gorgeous and enchanting as ever, her features were closed to him. She lingered in midair, suspended by her translucent wings.

"What are you doing *here*? Of all places?"

Atrox tried to get up, but could not. Something was holding him captive, and he was unable to get off the ground. "I'm coming to you."

She smiled sadly. "Why?"

His mouth opened, but no words came out. Was it his

impression, or did her shoulders slump?

"You think going through my father's challenges will really fix this? Fix us?"

"There is nothing to fix," Atrox said. "But I do believe it will give you the answer you've been searching for. The one I wasn't able to speak, before you left."

Catriona bit her lip. "Are you sure of this?"

Atrox scowled, not used to being so questioned. "I'm willing to try."

Catriona shook her head, turning it to the side as if refusing to let him see her face. "Go home, lover. This is not a quest you truly want to be on."

She faded away, fluttering her wings, and Atrox woke up with a start.

"Catriona!"

She was nowhere to be seen. Only the carcass lay, dead, and a reminder of the past he had once firmly shut behind a door. Now, it seemed Merlyddus was determined to make him relive his demons.

Not even thoughts of what would come was enough to deter him. He needed to see Catriona, to explain… To hear the real reason she left. And he would not exit this blasted realm until he got to her.

I only pray when I find her, that she will listen… Otherwise this will have been in vain.

With a disgusted scoff at his unusually dour mood, he got to his feet. Before proceeding to the next challenge, he looked behind and spoke softly. "If you're watching, or hearing me... I'm coming for you, my Fae queen."

CHAPTER 3

His left shoulder was still bleeding, leaving behind a trail of blood. Atrox stopped in his tracks when he noticed it and cursed under his breath.

"Fucking Vulper and his rage, and this damn king!"

He lifted his free hand, imbuing it with some of his divine energy, and watched as the wound cauterized, and the skin tied back together. Within moments, it was healed.

Guess I have access back to my abilities now that the challenge is done and over with. The thought didn't improve his mood.

Atrox picked up his sword again and continued walking through the ruins of his old palace. Merlyddus had said Catriona would be meeting him at the end of his journey, which meant there was nowhere to go but forward, and nothing to trust but his instincts.

Thoughts of her slowed down his gait, not that he could afford wasting time. Who knew how much of it had already gone by with his impromptu nap? But with each passing step in the world he'd once ruled, Atrox felt his chest tighten. The dream of Catriona had unsettled him.

For a long time, his only worry had been Vivienne's well-being. A charge was much easier to deal with – and care for – than a woman in her own, a Fae to boot. The more he thought about their last time together, the less he could figure out what had Catriona so upset. He had promised her an answer, and he wished it was an easy one, because he needed it.

Unless... Has it been staring me in the face this entire time? He stopped in his tracks, remembering one particular tidbit of their conversation. Something he had alluded to when speaking to Merlyddus.

"Talk to me." His whispered plea fell against her hair, even as he tightened his hold.

Catriona remained frozen in the embrace, not quite crying but trembling. Her words, when they came, hit him with the force of a tsunami. "Like you talked to me, about Merlin?"

Atrox pulled back enough to examine her expression. Though her features were taut, there was no anger in those eyes—only regret. And that hurt more than anything else.

"I meant to, I promise I did." When she looked away, he grabbed her chin between his thumb and index, forcing her to meet his gaze. "I swear."

"And why didn't you?" she countered.

"Because Merlin made me promise. He did not want you risking yourself, or for Carleigh to follow you here." He glanced around, taking in the destruction. "Evidently, we both had good intentions—and we both failed."

His secrecy had tainted their otherwise honest relationship, though Atrox had not meant it to. Merlin was Catriona's only sibling, and he'd been imprisoned far from them, with an explosive spell designed to take his life. Atrox had learned of the dilemma, but Merlin had chosen self-sacrifice, and Vivienne's well-being, over his own.

It had killed Atrox to let it go, but he had listened to his old friend. And then had hidden the fact from Catriona, telling only her father about it.

Had he really hurt her so bad? It seemed trivial, in comparison to what he had seen humans do, but perhaps his dishonesty had really broken her trust in him.

And if it had... *I refuse to believe this cannot be fixed.*

Determined, he started walking again, the echo of his footsteps resounding in the silence. He did not recall the entrance to his old stomping grounds being so long, nor so empty of spirits. The loneliness made him only more aware of his thoughts, annoying as they were. He had to make Catriona see the truth. That he'd never intended to break her trust, after all she had given him. That she meant more to him than...

I will find a way to settle this. For the first time in eons of existing, doubt clouded his mind.

And as it fogged his brain, refusing to allow other thoughts, or make his feet move forward, Atrox heard whispers around him.

Weak.

You are so....weak.

Weak....

At once, all dark ruminations of doubt escaped him and he straightened, tightening his grip on the sword. "Another monster this time?"

Monster?

A hiss, an echo, all around him.

Atrox glared at the darkness, even as the hairs on the

ATROX – AN AVALON CHRONICLES NOVELLA

back of his neck rose.

The only monster here....is you.

He lifted the sword, preparing to stop whatever attack in its tracks.

That won't do you any good.

Then it moved, lights flickered on the cavern walls and Atrox faced that which he had long ago forsaken – the darkness of the underworld. He should have known it would not let him off with a simple mark.

It appeared this time not in the shape of a seductress, but of a child. Half his size, with dark, inky hair and a chalky expression, it floated across the ground. With each movement, the shadows around its feet grew, as though they were tentacles.

Atrox took a step backwards. He had been around humans for too long, and the sight of a child – the thought of hurting one – brought bile to his throat.

As if sensing this, the creature laughed at him. "Weak..." The hiss was all around him.

Atrox narrowed his eyes. "You confuse me with another. There is no weak bone in my body, child. I used to rule this place."

The child hopped from spot to spot, its movements alien and unnatural. "*Used to*, is right."

Atrox's eyes narrowed on it. "And I defeated the creature who took my place. This means you owe me obedience."

Pale eyes, almost white, darkened with malice. "Owe? We do not owe you anything."

We?

Atrox glanced around himself, only then realizing there

was more than one child. They inched closer to him, circling him and tightening the space between them.

"What is it you want from me?"

"Your soul," the creature said simply.

Atrox laughed, and sneered at them. "My soul? Good luck with that. I am immortal."

More malicious laughter. "We marked you, fool."

"You will be ours, as the sands of time ever shift, and move forward."

Atrox's expression sobered, the mark on his shoulder taking on a new meaning. As did this attack. "You mean to delay me, to force me to lose these challenges so I am forever caught here." He paused, and the last missing piece fell in. "For you to feed off of."

"True," Darkness said.

Of course. Nothing like a powerful god to nourish its depraved tendencies. His grip tightened on the sword. "And what makes you think I'll give in easily?"

A young girl by his side laughed, though there was nothing endearing about it. The sound made his skin crawl, even more so when she said, "Will you really hurt us?"

Atrox spun to face her – and four others. Behind him, he registered more children stepping out from between the shadows. Though his grip on the sword tightened, he could not make himself swing it.

Shite.

They surrounded him and, same as the Faes earlier, they started closing in on him. Atrox dropped the sword, letting it fall to the dusty ground. He gritted his teeth, his eyes taking in the scene. *These children of darkness count on my mercy, my refusal to hurt them because of their youthful appearance... I need to make them reveal their true face, if I'm to properly fight them.*

Yet how could he do that?

Movement above him drew his eyes and he glanced up, too late. Another child that had been crawling the walls dropped on him, wrapping its tiny arms and legs around his neck and head like an octopus.

Atrox stumbled backwards, and tried to pull the creature away from him, but it latched on tightly. Remembering the strength he'd used against Vulper, he reached for the child's hands and tried to pry them apart – to no avail.

What in the devil....?

Oxygen was leaving him, and the creature seemed determined to choke him, its tiny legs cutting off his air supply. Atrox tried to think past the haze of asphyxiation, but something else entered his mind instead.

More doubt.

It crawled across his consciousness, removing all other thoughts. Catriona's hurt expression flashed in his mind, erasing everything else. Engrossed in the memory, it took him a moment to realize the child had moved off him, and he could breathe freely again.

And still, he was kneeling on the ground, his feet refusing to move. "What did you do to me?"

Child-like laughter surrounded him, and the first one who'd spoken stepped from the crowd. "Us? We did nothing that you were not already doing to yourself."

A young girl bounced across the ground to him, and stopped right in front of him. Blonde curls surrounded a face like Cupid's, with large eyes filled with malice. She grinned a toothy smile. "Liar, liar…"

Blinding pain shot through his head, and Atrox bent over, nearly touching the ground.

"And to think how easy it was!" The children's laughter echoed around him, but all he felt was the crippling pain, obliterating everything else – including his desire to wipe the floor with them.

≈ ♠ ≈

Atrox… Atrox…

The voice in his head was soft, feminine… familiar. It didn't take away the pain, but it did diminish it enough for him to realize something else was amiss.

You have to leave…

"I'm not…leaving…without you," he growled under his breath. Each word past his lips caused a stabbing pain in his head. He was not used to feeling so – human. And it left him unprepared for the attack.

Is this how I will go down? In front of children?

Anger filled him, rage at his hypocrisy. After calling Faitus a coward, here he was, unable to defend himself against younglings.

Leave, Atrox…

He gritted his teeth and grunted, pressing his forehead against the earth. It was no longer his pride at fault, but his heart. A flash of clarity hit him, remove some of the plaguing cobwebs. He knew why he missed Catriona, and it had nothing to do with her companionship or the amazing trysts. Rather, with the way she got him – the ambition in him, the power-hungry wolf – and never tried to change him.

"I'm. Not. Leaving." His voice was stronger, and though the stabbing pain was still present, Atrox managed to lift his head.

The laughter around him stopped abruptly, and the first child spoke again. "It is no use fighting it. Your weakness will end you."

Atrox smirked at the ground. "No." One last push, and he got himself up on his knees, back straight and eyes level with the astonished gaze of the creature.

"This… Cannot be!"

Atrox laughed – a dark, humorless chuckle. "You think you can own me, in a realm that used to be mine?" One knee lifted, then the other, and he was back to towering over the small faces.

"I am no weakling, especially not in my own domain." He held his hand out and his sword lifted off the ground, floating into his grip.

Then he lifted his free palm, and forced Darkness to shed away the illusion of children. Rather than their vulnerable forms, he was faced with tall, toothy creatures, twice his size, with gnarled hands and an odor fetid enough to make him retch.

Invigorated by the triumph, Atrox slashed the first one to bits, and it turned to dust. Then he turned to the next, and the next. They clawed at his back, or tried to, but he danced under their arms, refusing to be their puppet any longer.

Feet quick as lightning, strikes sure and fast, he didn't miss a single one. In the end, only the tallest creature was left standing. The leader. Atrox shoved the sword in his stomach with such force they both tumbled to the ground.

"How...did you....fight us?"

Atrox smirked. "The young girl called me a liar. It only made sense that my lies were what weighed me down. Specifically, the truth about my emotions, which I refused to face. Once I admitted them to myself, the rest was easy."

He pulled the blade free, and the creature blew away in a dusty cloud. His weapon was not spared either – it shriveled and disintegrated, the metal ruined by dark blood.

≈ ♠ ≈

"Not bad...for a fallen god."

Atrox blinked against the ground, then forced himself up on shaking arms. Panting, coughing, he glanced around for whoever had spoken. *Another foe?*

"Down here."

His gaze fell on a pixie-like creature, barely bigger than his thumb. Its entire body was tiny, green-skinned, with violet eyes. Strands of white hair stood atop its head like spikes, and it had the tiniest wings.

Once it had his attention, the tiny creature flew upwards until it was in front of his face. "I'm Ainsling."

Atrox narrowed his eyes on it. "Your kind don't live here. How did you get in?"

Ainsling sniffed. "If you must know, I was sent here."

"To keep an eye on me?"

When the pixie only stared at him, Atrox waved it off and got to his feet. "So the old man wants to witness my demise, does he? Well, I won't give him the satisfaction."

His gaze fell on the sword, broken and discarded to the side. With a sigh, he picked it up and ran his hand over it. Flames flushed, but the blade would not mend itself.

"You used it to defeat Darkness, and it has served its

purpose," Ainsling pointed out in a high-pitched voice.

Atrox scowled at the tiny creature. "Did anyone ask you for commentary?"

"No, but you are wasting time. And since you survived the challenge of brawn, and now brain, it would be a shame to see you lose the next."

Atrox took in the words, head tilted to the side. He crouched next to the creature again. "And you know what the next challenges are?"

"I do, but I will not tell you."

He snorted at the haughty tone and stood once more. "Of course not. Then be on your way back to the Fae realm, little one." Determined, he started walking again.

Out of the corner of his eye, he caught a buzz and something whizzing around his head. When he stopped, Ainsling flew in front of his face. "I have to accompany you."

Atrox rolled his eyes. "Suit yourself, but don't expect me to risk my life to save yours." To the walls, he hissed, "Let's see what you prepared next, old king."

CHAPTER 4

For hours, it seemed, Atrox walked through shadows and more shadows. He'd left the palace ruins behind long ago, and now trekked alongside more cavernous hallways that he did not remember. The mark on his arm throbbed, but he knew he had to keep going.

The pixie-like creature had floated around him and kept up with incessant chatter about the Fae world, until it had stopped. He'd been focused so much on moving forward that he didn't pay attention to it until only silence rang in his ears.

Recalling his earlier musings about loneliness, he squinted at his surroundings. "You still around?"

A pause, then, "Yes." It was a whispery, tired reply, and he narrowed his eyes on the ground around him, seeking, until he found the little thing panting.

I must have been walking much too fast for it to keep pace. That, paired with the pixie being a creature a light, in the underworld... No wonder it ran out of fumes.

Crouching, Atrox held out his hand to it, but Ainsling could not even move closer. "I warned you not to stay here," he said. "The underworld is no place for a tiny thing like you."

Violet eyes looked up with intensity. "What, because I'm a female?"

"Uh…" Atrox scratched the back of his neck. "Not quite, no. More that I don't want you to die, and Merlyddus to have yet another bone to pick with me."

Ainsling opened her mouth to speak, then shook her tiny head and pushed herself off the ground. "Why the rush, wolf god? Are you that eager to go to your death?"

His voice changed at that. "Merlyddus will not be the end of me, mark my words." He stood, dusting off his knees.

Leaving the pixie behind, Atrox started forward once more. Heat now scorched his skin, and the shirt he was wearing clung to him. With an annoyed sigh, Atrox pulled it off him and tossed it to the side.

The pixie made some sort of noise, and he looked around. She seemed to have gotten another influx of energy – or stubbornness – as she was floating in midair once more. Her horrified gaze was glued to his arm.

"What?" he asked.

"The… The mark. On your arm."

He'd almost forgotten about Darkness tattooing it on him – would it still stop him from exiting, now that he had defeated it? Would he survive, if he tried?

Atrox shrugged. "So what?"

"Is that why you are in a rush?" When he didn't answer, only kept going forward, the creature flew to his left side and yanked on a lock of his hair. "Answer me!"

Through gritted teeth, he said, "I am in no mood to speak."

"Really? Then what of Catriona? Are you in a mood to

speak about her?"

Atrox clenched his free fist, and continued walking.

"You really are a stubborn fool," Ainsling snorted.

"Stubborn?" His voice was low – a cold hiss – as he stopped and turned to face the creature. "*I'm* the stubborn one? She won't see me! I know I screwed up, but I had enough on my plate at the time, yeah? Would it kill her to give me a second chance, or do I have to beg forever to get one?"

Ainsling lifted a hand in warning. "Watch your tone when referring to my mistress."

"You. Asked."

After a moment of glaring, he turned to leave, but Ainsling was not done. "You should rest, wolf god. Marked or not, you cannot survive the next five challenges without something so essential as rest."

"Watch me," he growled.

In the next step, he stumbled, unaccustomed to the weakness coursing through him. "What else did Merlyddus bid you do, hmm? Spell me so I don't get out of here?"

Ainsling almost sounded hurt when she spoke. "He did not. I speak out of pure concern for your life."

Atrox shook his head, and continued walking. One moment he was putting one foot in front of the other, the next he toppled sideways and onto the ground, passed out.

≈ ♠ ≈

"You have to stop."

Atrox blinked in the darkness, only to be blinded by the light emanating from Catriona. She was bent over him, her hand caressing his cheek, locks of her flaming hair around him.

Her essence surrounded him, and his nostrils flared as

he smelled her around him. "I won't, not until I'm next to you again."

Her blue eyes darkened with sadness, the light he was used to seeing, gone. She dropped her touch from his cheek, and he felt the loss in his very soul. One hand, weakened by his ordeals, lifted to her.

Atrox hated that it trembled with emotion, but when he touched her creamy skin, all other thoughts mattered less. "Tell me, beautiful Fae, do you really think you can resist what is between us?"

His eyes glinted when they noticed her hesitation, the parting of her lips – as if unable to help herself. "Let me remind you what we had, darling one."

The hand on her cheek shifted to grasp her nape, and drag her mouth to his. Atrox reined in his need to control, and instead pulled at her lips like a violin's strings, tugging and sucking on the top and bottom lip until she was opening for him, moaning, both her hands going to his chest.

Then Catriona pulled back, shaking her head, and disappeared.

≈ ♠ ≈

"Catriona!" Like before, he woke up screaming her name, but it was violet eyes he landed on. Atrox wiped the water off his face and lifted to an upright position. "What did you do to me?"

"I? Nothing! But you should have listened to me and rested. Your body gave way."

Atrox glared at the pixie-like creature. "Would you get off my back already, you little shit?"

The thing had the nerve to look offended. "I will not!

And I would advise you to watch your tone with me."

"Or what?" Atrox snorted.

Ainsling shot a blast of something at his foot, and Atrox yelped and stepped back. "What the–"

"You may look down on me, ye fallen god, but I have power you have no idea of."

Atrox's eyes narrowed. "Fine. Be a spy."

He stood to continue onwards, well aware the pixie was once more fluttering around his shoulder and following him. The heat increased as they travelled, turning each breath into agony. As they made it around another corner, a shadow moved in the depths of the cavern.

Atrox clenched his fist, regretting the loss of his sword. "Who goes there?"

The shadow shuffled further. "You don't recognize an old friend?"

His jaw went slack at the voice. "Merlin? How?"

The wizard was not in his usual old man disguise, rather in his regular appearance with striking blue eyes, and hair dark enough to be almost purple in the bare light surrounding them. He wore his usual grey robes, and gripped a staff in his right hand.

"Thought you might use the help, old friend."

Shaking his head, Atrox stepped closer and clasped his hand in his, then clapped Merlin on the back.

"I appreciate the offer, but I'm running out of time."

Merlin's eyes shifted to the mark on his arm, and he nodded. "Seems like it, I'd say." He turned to the rest of the hallway, and gestured for Atrox to follow him. "Come with me, I have a shortcut."

"Don't go," the pixie whispered in his ear, but Atrox ignored her.

"Shortcut to where?" he asked as he followed the wizard.

"Where you need to be." A side-glance later, Merlin grinned. "You must be tired, too. I can start a bonfire while you get some rest."

Atrox snorted. "It's not heat we lack here."

"The fire is not for heat, but to keep away the creatures roaming around here."

Atrox nodded, and off they went again. After a beat, he said, "Vivienne and Sébastien are fine, if you're wondering."

"I knew they would be." His voice was detached, and the wolf god presumed it was to keep a certain distance from his pupil given their recent issues.

Still, something nagged at him. Again, the pixie said, "Stop following him," and again he ignored her, instead flicking her off his shoulder.

After a few moments, they stopped in a junction of the hallway, and Merlin pointed to a corner. A fire grew, inviting and warm. It made the air even hotter, but Atrox forced himself to sit opposite it.

Merlin's right, there is nowhere safe here.

The bonfire roared, and the pixie creature was quiet in her corner. Atrox turned to his friend of old. "How did you ever survive Carleigh's trickery, and Morgana?"

"That sorcerer was never a match for me," Merlin grinned. "As for Morgana, you should know. You told her to wish me a good life, did you not?"

Atrox chuckled under his breath. "And so I did." Silence

lengthened between them again. Then Merlin spoke, his tone different.

"Did you ever think about what could have been?"

"Hmm?"

"It was with my powers that you escaped the curse your siblings put on you. Imagine how it could have gone differently, with me by your side, if you wished that rebellion again."

"What, and turn out the old pantheon?" Atrox snorted. "Been there, done that."

Merlin's eyes were intense. "But you could have succeeded this time. *We* could have. It's not too late."

Atrox tilted his head. "I heard you the first time."

"Perhaps you didn't."

The wolf god took in Merlin's feverish gaze, the pressing tone of his voice, and finally clued in. There was nothing normal about the conversation, not when Merlin himself had learned the price of ambition in the past.

He stood, putting some distance between them. "You're not Merlin."

The mage in front of him stayed frozen, then smirked in a way he'd never seen the real wizard do. "Took you long enough. But I'm afraid you'll need more than sheer will to banish me."

Atrox continued to step away, until his back hit the cavernous wall. He dug his hand in it, and with his entire being called forth the power that had once been his. The earth rumbled, the walls shook, then a patch of ground rose up like a small tower.

Atrox punched it, and broken dirt fell to the side, revealing a new sword. He gripped the hilt wrapped in black leather and pulled it out. "We'll see about that."

For a second, he wondered if the same rules as with Vulper applied here. Things seemed to change with each new challenge, and he really hoped he would be able to reach his divine powers. Having fought Merlin in the past, he knew the wizard was a formidable opponent.

And whether or not this one was truly Merlin, the same risks still applied.

Buzzing by the side of his face confused him. Then Ainsling said, "What are you doing?"

Out of the corner of his mouth, Atrox said, "About to fight a friend, what's it look like?"

He waved his hand as he would at a fly. "Get out of my way, and find cover. This won't be pretty."

Merlin took his time standing, maintaining a cool expression the entire time. He'd known the wizard for ages, and never had he seen such an expression on his face. It was even more confirmation that this man was not his friend – nowhere close to it, in fact.

"You're a hypocrite, you know?" The wizard laughed.

They circled each other, Atrox holding the sword, Merlin gathering magic in his hands. For all intents and purposes, it still looked like the real thing. *Maybe this is some illusion, or another creature.*

Regardless, Atrox felt for his divine energy and flames licked the sword in his hands. It flamed, then settled into a light blue glow. Merlin's eyes narrowed on it, and he scowled. Then he released the jet of magic in his hands, tossing it towards the wolf god.

Atrox lifted the blade and cut through the magic. A rush

of relief escaped him at the realization he was, in fact, allowed to use his powers this time around. More determined, he closed the distance between them as Merlin kept throwing magic from each side towards him.

One such giant ball he hit, but it didn't disintegrate. Rather, it reformed and struck again. Atrox parried it again, but it was a stubborn thing, with a will of its own. As his attention was occupied by it, Merlin spoke.

"With your godly powers and my Fae, we can start a new rebellion. Make both your pantheon and my kinsmen hiding on their secret realm, our pawns. You're telling me you really don't wish that any more?"

Atrox spared him a glare, before ducking the ball of magic again. "Yeah, that's exactly what I'm saying."

"I don't believe it," Merlin said. His eyes shone with a familiar blue glimmer. "You were born for greatness, Atrox."

Grunting at the stupid orb, the wolf god warred with it. Merlin was distracting him, in the hopes of making his baser self admit to something that was simply no longer a truth. Shaking his head, he said, "So were many human kings. And queens. Does not mean I need that power in order to be happy."

"Happy?" Merlin choked. "Since when do you care about such trivial things?"

Atrox finally managed to cut through the orb, for good this time. He turned and faced Merlin, a faint sheen of sweat covering his body. "Since I met Catriona, fool. And whether you are the real Merlin or not, you must have felt the same with Morgana. I now understand this."

His admission gave the wizard pause, and he tilted his head to the side. "After so long spent keeping us apart, you tell me this?"

Atrox shrugged. "Your love was destructive, it is true. But I understand what made you so protective of it, and why you kept making the same mistake, over and over again. I feel the same about Catriona, and I need you to get out of my way so I can get to her."

Merlin shook his head. "Afraid that is not possible, old friend."

The wolf god lifted the sword again, inhaling a deep breath. "In that case, I am sorry." With a roar, he closed the rest of the distance and kicked Merlin's staff out of his hand, then shoved the sword in his stomach.

Closing his eyes, he whispered again to the darkness. "Greed no longer rules me, my friend. Only love has that power."

When he pulled the sword out of him, Merlin's image became deformed, with drooping jaws, sunken eyes, and skin that looked like broken leaves. The creature, whatever it was, dropped to the ground and practically melted into a puddle, leaving Atrox staring in shock.

CHAPTER 5

Atrox gazed for a beat longer at what had masqueraded as his friend, then dropped his sullied sword and exhaled heavily. "Is there no one I can trust here?" he muttered.

"I warned you not to follow him."

Atrox turned his glare to Ainsling. The pixie had flown back in the air, and was looking at the puddle with a mixture of disgust and fear on her face.

"What was that thing?"

The pixie shrugged and fluttered her wings in front of him. "Does it matter?"

"It does to me. That wizard is my friend... Did I, or did I not, just kill him?"

Ainsling sighed, and floated closer to stare Atrox in the eye. "You already know it was not him, wolf god. He represented your challenge for greed."

Atrox straightened and wiped a hand over his brow. His entire body was sweating, the heat surrounding him making it worse. "Greed? First strength, then intelligence, now greed? What, exactly, are these challenges supposed to prove?"

"Have you truly not realized it yet?"

Atrox thought back to the beginning, and his conversation with Merlyddus. Truth be told, he'd been much too busy trying to survive the challenges than actually think of their purpose. Now that he did, it took him only a momentary lapse to realize it.

"He wants me to prove my worth, to be Catriona's suitor."

"Well done," Ainsling praised, her voice riddled with sarcasm. "Only, it is not to Catriona you must prove your worth, but to him."

Atrox narrowed his eyes. "Everything I do, I do for her."

Gripping the new blade, he pushed past the pixie, in his haste nearly crushing her.

"Watch it!"

"What!" Atrox snarled. "I've just about had it with you! Go and tell your king I'm doing his damned quest, will you?"

Ainsling looked at him. "It is not the king I serve, you stubborn fool."

Atrox stared. "Who, then?"

"Catriona."

He blinked, thinking he hadn't heard properly. "I'm sorry, what?"

"I serve Her Majesty."

He gritted his teeth. "And you couldn't have mentioned that before!" Atrox wanted to squeeze the foolish being until she begged for release.

Before he could, fog surrounded and separated them.

"Who goes there now?" He was getting tired of games. Where the hell was Catriona!

"One whose name you should remember."

Atrox held back a groan. "I should've known you'd be next, after Merlin."

Morgana stepped out of the shadows, her long raven hair tumbling down her back. She was dressed in a burgundy gown that fell off her shoulders. Her grey eyes glittered with the power she used. "You should have, yes."

Her cold smile was the only warning, before she blasted Atrox into the closest cavern wall. And it all crumbled around him.

≈ ♠ ≈

Catriona was there again, he knew it without opening his eyes. Her scent surrounded him, and the cool breeze on his cheeks was an indication he was no longer in the bowels of the underworld.

"Atrox, open your eyes!"

Her urgent tone got to him, and he blinked. A blood red sunrise coated the sky, turning to pure flames the red hue of her hair.

"Couldn't stay away, my Fae queen?" Atrox lifted a hand to her cheek, but Catriona shrank away, shaking her head.

"Why do you insist on putting yourself through this?"

Her tone was a cold shower, and he got to an upright position. His head felt foggy, heavy, like he'd been…

"A cavern crumbled atop of you," Catriona whispered, reading his expression. "You may be a god, but in this trial, there are limits even to your endurance."

Atrox snorted and went to stand – immediately regretting it. He swayed and nearly toppled over, but Catriona slid under his arm and kept him from falling. Something settled in him at having her so close, within his reach, despite the dizziness affecting him.

"Are you determined to die on me?"

Atrox shifted then, peering down at the Fae in his arms. She refused to meet his gaze, and half his weight rested on her. He felt better now, more stable, but wasn't about to show it if it meant losing the closeness.

"No," he said, "only determined to get to you."

Catriona inhaled sharply then, and looked up at him. Her blue eyes shone with hope, impossible to ignore this close by.

"You forgave me once before," Atrox whispered, keeping his voice low, to keep her enthralled. "When I chose reincarnation, to watch over Vivienne once more. But that part of my life is done, and now I am free to do as I wish. Will you not forgive me one last time, for being a fool?"

Catriona's lips parted, and that electricity he was so accustomed to between them, was his undoing. Atrox shifted once more, saw the panic flare in her eyes, and they both toppled to the ground. He cushioned her fall with his arms, but made sure she was caged between his body and the earth, unable to escape.

"Atrox…"

A corner of his mouth turned upwards into a roguish grin. "Allow me, my Fae queen…to worship at your feet."

He kissed down the side of her neck, even as his hands roamed everywhere. Catriona was fire underneath him, writhing and begging for more. He knew that if he could just show her, through his actions, she would understand…

But she started fading under him, and he looked up in a panic to see her distraught expression.

≈ ♠ ≈

"Time to wake up, wolf god."

The voice was in his ear, unfamiliar – at least for a moment. Then he recognized the revenge-filled tone, and blinked his eyes open. Rage filled him – at being imprisoned, at having been so close to get through to Catriona.

Morgana stood in front of him, surrounded by dust and fog. Her robes were not touched by the dust, and her grey eyes shone brighter still, of a light he knew meant nothing good. Black hair fell past her waist, and her features were set in a mask of stone. Only a cruel smile played on her lips, which alone warned Atrox of what was in store for him.

"Morgana." His head throbbed as he spoke, the vibrations of his voice only making things worse. When he tried to move, he discovered he'd been bound to what remained of the cavern's wall, with chains that dug into his wrists.

When he tried to break them, he hissed at the pain scorching his wrists. "What is this sorcery?"

Morgana paced in front of him, tapping her chin with her index finger. "Something to keep you stuck here, at my mercy. At least until I am done with you."

Atrox bared his teeth. "You aren't real, same as Merlin."

She was on him in a breath, her nails digging into his neck. "Do. Not. Speak. That. Name."

They glared at each other, then she let him go. Atrox could feel droplets of blood drip down his chest, but he didn't bother looking down to confirm. Instead, his eyes surreptitiously checked the surroundings to see if Ainsling was anywhere. The pixie had disappeared.

I hope she's not stuck beneath the rubble. If nothing else, he didn't want a loyal servant of Catriona's hurt.

"Now," Morgana said and drew his attention once more, "I will tell you a story. And in the end, you will reveal why it is you decided to intervene in something that was none of your business, and destroyed my life."

"I did not–"

Morgana jerked her wrist, and the chains binding him dug more into his flesh. Atrox gritted his teeth, settling his onyx glare on the sorceress. "Fine. Do your worst."

"Once upon a time, there was a little princess. She'd been born of a Fae, and an evil man who wished to control the Fae. As the child grew, she realized she had power – *a lot* of power, enough to rule the kingdom. But another came into her life, a man who was both her salvation and her destruction. While he curbed her urges, he also taught her how to use the magic. And, in the end, he took everything from her."

Morgana's eyes glittered with malice. "This man would not have entered the kingdom, were it not for a god who decided to back him up. A wolf demon, a fallen deity who instead of sticking to what he was supposed to do – *corrupt* – decided to befriend the wizard."

She stepped closer to Atrox, her hand raised, a light shining within it. "My question to you, wolf god, is why? Why did you support Merlin? What was so special about him, that you turned your back on the underworld that was yours, in order to help him?"

The sorceress may have been an illusion, something created by the Fae king, but the emotions in her eyes and voice were quite real. Atrox thought back to the last time he'd seen the real Morgana, to the wistful look in her eyes as she'd lost her son, lost the battle, and decided to leave Uther's kingdom.

His thoughts then turned to Merlin, and their eons of friendship – of rivalry. They had had both, over the course of centuries, but despite their misgivings a deep bond of friendship had tied them together. Above all, they had both wanted Arthur's future realized, and Vivienne's. They had worked together for that goal.

But in the beginning… What was it that had pulled him to the wizard?

Atrox lifted his gaze to Morgana's. "Honesty is what you want, yes? This challenge is meant to show I am not truthful, that I lie to get my way." His gaze rose higher, to the ceiling. "You could have picked better, Merlyddus!"

"Could he have, though?" Morgana asked in a soft voice, unlike her. "Out of all the lives you crossed, can you honestly say there was another whose future was more fucked up than mine because of your actions?"

"Not mine alone, Morgana," Atrox said.

"You will blame others for the part you played?"

A muscle ticked in his jaw. "I will take ownership for my part, for not doing enough to stop Merlin. I should have been less concerned about following the rules of my pantheon and more about doing the right thing. And I did amend that, in the end."

Morgana only pursed her lips, watching him with an inscrutable gaze.

"But it was not all my fault. You had freedom of choice, as did Merlin. And when I tried to stop things from progressing, neither of you listened to me." Atrox sighed. "Do you not remember when I begged you not to take that ultimate step, to hurt those men in the woods?"

It had been after she and Merlin had parted ways. Atrox had tried to go after her, only to find her ready to kill some men that been ready to attack her. Knowing how Fae magic worked and the effect it would have on her, Atrox had tried to convince Morgana not to kill them.

The memory of that day – the conversation – rang in his head, leaving a bitter taste in his mouth.

"Do not give me that. You know what they wanted to do to me!" she yelled, features contorted in fury.

Atrox stepped nearer, trying to get in her mind.

"If you come any closer, I will snuff out their worthless lives like candles."

"Why, Morgana?"

"Because Merlin betrayed me. Because he took away our most precious gift, and ruined our future!"

"These three do not have to pay for his mistakes."

Atrox knew it was the wrong thing to say the minute Morgana stilled.

"No," she smiled coldly. "But they will regardless."

Morgana could have left it at a warning. But seeing the men's repulsive faces, sensing what they had planned to do to her... She gritted her teeth and watched as the obscurity consumed them.

Atrox shook his head to clear it, though he could have sworn seeing echoes of the conversation in her eyes. Or was that his imagination?

"Morgana, you made the wrong choice then. Don't do the same now."

She took a step closer to him, pointing an index, and a trail of fire scorched down his chest. Atrox gritted his teeth against the pain, refusing to cry out again.

"You can torture me all you like," he said, "but none of that will bring your child back. None of it will take the pain away."

"One thing will," she said. "Your admission of guilt."

Atrox looked at her then, *really* looked at her. "I am guilty, but of not doing more. I hid the truth from myself, refused to see it for what it was."

Morgana grimaced. "That's not all!"

"What, then? What is it you want me to apologize for?" His voice was hoarse from holding back the cries of anguish she craved to rip from him.

The sorceress paced from side to side, muttering under her breath. Atrox tried to yank at his chains, and thought he felt them give more than usual. The mark on his shoulder throbbed, warning him once more of the time elapsed.

Morgana faced him then, her face set in stone. "The death of an innocent."

"What?"

"That is what you need to ask penance for."

Atrox thought back to eons ago, when Merlin had met Morgana, and all the events that had led to her downfall. One, in particular, stood out. And in that moment, he knew he'd finally found the solution to get out of the cuffs.

"You mean Uther, and what Merlin did to help him get Ygraine. What led, in the end, to the birth of Arthur."

Morgana scowled, her face growing darker, a snarl passing her lips. Atrox nodded, as if thinking hard about it. She slapped him, but still he said nothing.

"Speak!" she finally shouted in his face.

Atrox met her gaze then. "Merlin came up with the ruse of his own, I had nothing to do with it. And while I feel guilt for what happened to you, I will not take responsibility for something that was not my choice."

Blood tricked over his chest, and the gashes closed. Atrox jerked against the restraints, finally collapsing one. He realized why – with each truth he said, her hold on him lessened.

"You were right, Morgana," he said. "It was power that drove me to Merlin, power that initially united us in our quest. And I tried to stop him, perhaps my intervention did not give the right results… But I *tried* to stop him from helping Uther, from everything else. I saw what would come, and was unable to avoid it."

The words were ripped from his throat, but with them, a heavy burden lifted off his shoulders. "Is that what you wanted? The full, honest, truth? Despite my lord of the underworld status, and all my godly powers, I was outmatched by something way more basic – friendship. And the care I took for that blasted wizard."

He yanked against the chains once more, and this time was released and fell into a crouch. He straightened to his full height, clenching his fists. The sorceress stood in front of him, mouth agape.

"That is the truth. Perhaps not the one you wished to hear, but the one I lived through."

With one whoosh of his hand, fire ignited another sword for him to use. This time, Atrox did not hesitate. He drew the weapon and sliced through the creature, who turned to smoke in front of his very eyes.

"I can only hope, wherever you did end up, that you

found peace, sorceress."

Atrox looked around then, and coughed at the remaining dust. "Ainsling? Are you still here?"

When nothing answered him, he shrugged. "Figured the pixie would run away at the second hint of trouble."

Something hit the back of his head then – hard. Atrox groaned and brought his hand to the throbbing spot, only to, draw it away showing blood. He turned around and met violet, angry eyes.

"And here I was just starting to like you!"

Atrox snorted. "And I, you. Not." Then he turned to the hallway, frowning at the path laid before them, half covered in rubble. "Where to, now?"

Head held high, Ainsling fluttered past him and pointed in the distance. With a sigh, Atrox followed.

I'm getting closer, Catriona.

CHAPTER 6

Despite being underground – or so he thought – Atrox felt like he'd been walking for ages. His feet, for the first time in eons, actually hurt, as did his various wounds that were still healing.

Something about the air here interferes with my ability to recuperate.

Something or some*one*. He had no doubt Merlyddus was probably enjoying every bit of the show, and constantly thought of ways to make his challenges harder. Not being able to heal would count as such a way.

"Are you feeling alright?"

Ainsling's voice by his ear jerked him to a stop, and Atrox glanced around. He'd ended up at a crossroads, facing two tunnels. Only one could be picked, he knew, but he was having a hard time focusing on anything at all.

Swaying, he swung the sword – narrowly missing the pixie – and tried to use it as a crutch to stand. Only, it wobbled under him and fell away, removing his last support. It didn't take him long to lose the last of his energy. One moment he was walking, then he stumbled and nearly impaled himself on the sword as he hit the wall.

Ainsling flew in his face, the violet eyes narrowed in concern. "What's gotten into you?"

Atrox shook his head, trying to speak, but his mouth was pasty and the words came out slurred. "Morgana…" Whatever he tried to say was lost as he dropped to the ground, and into darkness.

≈ ♠ ≈

"Enjoying yourself, wolf god?"

Atrox found himself in the middle of a foggy forest. It smelled like sulfur, and something about the energy raked him as...wrong.

"Who goes there?"

His question went unanswered at first, then the mist parted to reveal Merlyddus himself. The king had his staff in hand, and he gave Atrox a condescending smile. "And here I thought you would be easy to get rid of."

"Rid of?" Atrox snorted. "Which part of my demand did you ignore, king? I'm not leaving here without Catriona."

"You won't be leaving, period."

Atrox tossed his sword to the side, and spread his arms. "Really? I've so far succeeded in your challenges. I defeated Vulper showing my strength, bypassed Darkness showing my intelligence, and survived both Merlin and Morgana's likenesses, demonstrating my lack of greed and my honesty. Which, of that exactly, tells you I'm failing?"

Merlyddus chuckled, as if amused. "You twist my words, wolf god. I never said you were failing. Have you not understood yet? Whether you succeed or not, you still won't be leaving this prison."

Atrox clenched his fists. "And why not? What is it you have against me?"

"Besides breaking my daughter's heart?"

The confirmation did something to Atrox. He'd seen it in Catriona's eyes, but had forced himself to push past it, not to let the guilt get to him. Now, it throbbed in his chest, spreading through him, and removing some of his arrogance.

"It was not my intention," he whispered.

Merlyddus was having none of it. Like a king possessed, eyes flashing, his calm demeanor was lost. The mask gone, his tone was cutting ice. "As if I needed more reason, you are a *god*. A foolish deity, prone to corruption, to ambition – there is nothing good in you, nothing worth saving."

"Catriona saw something," Atrox said. "Why else would she help me lift my siblings' curse, and become myself once more?"

Merlyddus laughed, though it was not humorous – rather bitter, empty. "She took pity on you, fool! Your kind and ours is not meant to mix. There is a reason we were at war. We cannot cohabitate, because you will not respect our laws, and Faes do not bow down to inferior beings."

"Inferior?" Atrox snorted. "Isn't that a tad much? You take liberty with your words, king. Less careful now that you don't have an entourage?" His eyes narrowed. "To be fair, why are we here? What do you get out of this?"

"Taunting you," Merlyddus said. "Making sure you know you will never get out of here, let alone get to my daughter. I have vowed to keep you away."

Knowing how strong Fae magic was, Atrox inhaled sharply. "You had best not made such a vow out loud, fool."

Merlyddus' eyes flashed. "Fool? Watch yourself, mongrel."

Something snapped inside Atrox. He had been following the rules, behaving himself, and still the king was nowhere close to accepting his feelings for Catriona. The rejection stung, but the insolence was what really got to him.

Head bowed, he tried to take a deep breath, to quiet the racing of his pulse, but it was too late. There was a reason his brooch – his symbol in the old pantheon – was a wolf, a reason his demon form chose that same animal. Something in Atrox, deep down, was primal and impulsive and...

Fuck this shite.

He lifted his head and Merlyddus narrowed his eyes. Atrox knew what he was seeing. A hardening of his features, clenching of his jaw – and fists – and the glare of his eyes becoming red as power flowed through him.

"You want to do it the hard way, king?" Atrox smirked. "Then let us fight it out. And when you are kneeling in front of me, barely alive, I will remind you of your words - and offer you enough mercy to take them back."

Merlyddus pointed his staff towards Atrox, but he was quicker. Divine power flowed from his hands, unbidden, unchallenged, slamming into the king. The staff offered him protection – to some extent. But just as Fae magic was primal, fuelled by emotions, so could Atrox's divine energy be. And his desire to be with Catriona, his rage at being apart, was grand. Too grand to contain.

A flash of something crossed Merlyddus' face, even as Atrox heard a distinct crack in the staff. He smirked, and stepped closer – but something was already pulling him back.

"Remember this," he told the king as he lowered his hand. "Remember it *well* the next time you decide to invade my dreams."

≈ ♠ ≈

Atrox woke up, squinting at the shadows. The pixie was poking him – that was what had woken him up. He stood, glaring at it. "What are you interrupting my sleep for?"

Ainsling only squeaked and pointed.

Slowly, Atrox looked around – and scrambled to his feet. But the sword was kicked out of his reach, and he found himself staring down the tip of another. He clenched his jaw. "Come to get your revenge at last, brother?"

Aequus stepped out of the darkness, proving he was, indeed, holding a sword to his neck. A toga covered his body, held up with a panther brooch. A lock of hair dropped over his emerald eyes, a smirk on his lips. "Revenge, brother? My, and I thought Earth cured you of your arrogance."

Atrox took a step forward as if to hit, but the sword cut into his skin. "Ah, ah. Watch yourself."

Silence lengthened as they glared each other, no love lost. Long ago, it had been Aequus who'd thrown Atrox out of the skies. But therein did not lie his biggest fault. Rather, him and Ardea, their sister, had decided to let Atrox's old lover, Deasa, die.

He held Deasa's body tighter to him, before turning his head to the side towards Ardea.

"I have never asked you for anything," Atrox murmured hoarsely, "since my childhood years, but now I do. Not for me, but for another. I no longer have the strength to aid her, but you do. Help Deasa!"

Ardea moved closer, but Aequus' hand restrained her. She looked to her brother in shock, but met only stone in his expression. "No. Punishment was already doled out. It must be the fates' command Deasa dies in this way."

The memory of that day, despite the eons, was as fresh as ever in his mind, as was his desire for revenge. He had never forgiven them.

"Enough."

The voice was softer, but tinged with ruthlessness. Atrox glanced over his shoulder. Ardea stepped out of the shadows behind him, her unique eyes focused on him – one black, one green. As usual, she had her hawk brooch on, holding the toga over her right shoulder.

A second time, in as many days? What are the odds... He had thought it odd she came to visit him before the challenges, to warn him, but now he knew there must be more to it.

"Are you both apparitions, or did you really deign to come in the underworld?" Atrox asked.

Ardea's lips twitched. "Underworld?"

Aequus was not so subtle, rather throwing his head back and flat-out laughing. It made Atrox straighten to his full height, fists clenched. Ainsling flew by his ear, and her whisper carried to him.

"Do you know them?"

"Unfortunately," Atrox said. "They're my siblings."

Ainsling's gaze travelled over both gods, then she floated closer still to his ear. "Given your *friends* ended up being your enemies, am I to assume the same will happen with your so-called family?"

A snort escaped him, and he lifted the shoulder she perched on in a shrug. "Probably. You had best take cover." Ainsling took flight, and he turned his attention to his siblings. "What, exactly, amuses you so?"

"Have you lost your touch on Earth, brother, or did you become simple-minded?"

Atrox growled, his entire aura darkening. "Drop that sword, and I'll show you how simple-minded I am."

Ardea rolled her eyes and stepped within his field of vision, interrupting his squabble with Aequus. "Enough with the confrontations. Yes, we have come here, but it is not the underworld around us."

An undercurrent ran through him at her words, but already he was shaking his head. "You lie."

"No. We are your kin, if you have forgotten. It is the king of Faes who lied."

Atrox glared at them. "So why have you come? To laugh some more? Turning me into a dog for a lifetime wasn't enough?"

Ardea sighed, and lowered her gaze to the ground. "It was uncalled for. A prank that lasted much longer than should have, and by the time I tried to reverse it, Morgana had taken hold of you."

Atrox growled. "Because you weakened me. Need I remind you that you purposefully ensured I reincarnated as a canine, in order to have your eternal laugh at my expense?"

The two gods shared a look, and Aequus finally dropped the sword. "We are sorry, brother. And we know what you did for us."

Atrox turned away. This must be another ploy, and he

was nowhere stupid enough to fall into admitting what he had done, only to lose everything once more. Not when he had another challenge to get through.

Voice taut with tension, he hissed, "Don't know what you mean."

"You killed Vulper."

Atrox stopped in his tracks. Then, he laughed darkly. "So that's why you're here. To get a confession, and force me to pay?"

He turned to face them, opening his arms. "Well, have at it, my dear siblings." Taking a step closer, he hardened his tone. "You should be worshipping at my feet for having saved you. We all know the pantheon was in disarray after you discovered Vulper's duplicity. You both came and *begged me* to do something about it."

Aequus' cheeks reddened, and Ardea looked away at the reminder. A humorless chuckle escaped him. "And so it happened my interests finally aligned with yours, and now you wish to punish me for it? A bit late, isn't it?"

"Atrox, we –" Ardea started, but stopped when he lifted his palm.

"I wasn't done, sister. For the record, I did nothing wrong. Merlin's Fae powers intervened with your curse, and our own rules. You both know what happens when Faes and gods mix." He shrugged. "He gave me the power to go against you. And I shed my identity after. I paid for my sins, and redeemed myself. It was Gaia herself who returned my full self."

Ardea's eyes widened and she shared a shocked look with Aequus. "Gaia? The Supreme Goddess?"

Atrox only arched an eyebrow. "Is there another one?"

When their silence lengthened, and the mark on his arm throbbed, he said, "Listen, if you're here to punish me, you're a bit late."

Ardea shook her head. "No, that's not why-"

His eyes glittered black onyx. "Then you either get out of my way, or fight me."

"We are not here to fight," Aequus said.

The sword still in his hand said different. And given Atrox still had a bone to pick with them, he wasn't about to let this opportunity pass him by.

"I don't believe a single word out of your mouth. And even if you aren't here for punishment, this is too good to pass up on." Atrox didn't hesitate, and let loose a blast of light.

It hit Aequus smack in the chest, sending him sprawling in the darkness, his sword landing somewhere else. Ardea stepped where he had been, holding up her hand to defend. "Atrox, wait!"

Another blast left him, rage suffusing him. It had been their choices that had robbed him of Deasa. They had tossed him out of his home, his pantheon, and left him to rot. For eons, all they had done was intervene with his life, and make it worse.

Now that he had them at his mercy? He was not about to let them go.

Killing another god would have been pushing it, given what Gaia had done for him. But who said he could not return some of the punishment they had doled on him a while back?

As ideas swam in his head, his vision darkened and he stepped towards them. One hand held his sword, the other blasts of light. Fury ruled him, yes…

"Atrox!" The tiny voice was in his ear, but he had no

time to listen. He had to take this chance, to hurt them as they had him.

"Atrox, don't!" Ainsling tried again, this time flying in his face. His vision was blurry, but then it focused on the pixie.

"What...?"

"You cannot hurt your siblings," Ainsling said. "They're real! I sense their divine energy – there is no way Merlyddus could have faked it. This is another test, designed to make you lose all that you have gained... You must resist it!"

"A test...?" Fog once more filled his mind, and no matter how he tried to fight it, Atrox felt it crawl over him, taking over his actions. His hand tightened on the hilt of the sword, his muscles clenching in anticipation.

A roar from the shadows took him by surprise and he whirled around, parrying another blade just in time. Aequus' emerald gaze was filled with rage, his jaw tense and nostrils flaring.

"Here we come to make peace, and you attack us?"

He pulled back the sword, only to swing it once more. Atrox blocked it again and felt the vibrations run through his arms, and into his shoulders. He had forgotten how much stronger physically his brother was.

Sparks flew in the air as their swords clashed again – and again. Ainsling cried out warnings, but Atrox was deaf to them. In one particular move, he ducked under Aequus' blade and swung his leg out, tripping him. The larger god cursed under his breath as he fell backwards.

Then Atrox's sword was at his throat, and he held up his palms. The fury in his eyes dimmed, replaced by a flicker of fear. "Brother, we truly came here in peace. Please."

"He speaks the truth."

Without looking behind, Atrox shifted to the side so he could hold Ardea in his view. "And what makes you think I would believe you?"

It was then he noticed her cheeks were bathed by tears. "We have done you harm, Atrox, and we apologise for it. Truly. Do not give up what took you so long to recover, only for the sake of revenge against us."

Something nagged at the back of his mind. A memory of them as children laughing, chasing each other in gardens of flowers. His grip on the sword slackened, then he tightened it again and shook his head.

"Are you doing this?" His glare only met Ardea's confused stare.

"She is not. I am."

He glanced to the side, to Ainsling who was floating closer.

"Damn pixie," Atrox cursed, rubbing his left temple. "Get out of my head!"

"My mistress would not want you doing something you would regret. Especially not when it is due to her father's mind tricks."

Atrox glanced back at his brother, then his sister. His hand trembled again. Something was pushing him to take his revenge, but he was fighting it. "You're really here? You are no illusions?"

Ardea shook her head. "We are here, Atrox."

He closed his eyes, then with a huge effort of will, lowered the sword from Aequus. His brother breathed a sigh of relief, but stood motionless.

Panting, Atrox wiped at his brow. "So you're really here to mend fences?"

A wry smile on her lips, Ardea nodded. "Yes, brother."

He glanced between them, then straightened to his full height, extending a hand to Aequus. His brother took it and rose to his feet.

"I'm sorry," he said simply.

Aequus grasped his tighter. "You have nothing to apologize for. Let bygones be bygones, and let us start anew."

Atrox stared between them, realizing what this meant. "You are offering me my home back?"

"If you so wish it," Ardea said.

"*After* you get your Fae queen," Aequus added with a smirk. As a second thought, he rubbed his cheek and said, "She really packs a punch when she wants to."

His confusion must have shown, as Aequus laughed. "I've had the pleasure of meeting Catriona. She came looking for you, and I might have pushed the wrong buttons."

Ardea laughed. "What he means is, she clawed his face."

Something in his chest felt both heavy and light. Atrox rubbed the spot, even as Ainsling perched on top of his marked shoulder. "You have to keep going," she whispered. "Time is running out."

Ardea came to the side, noticing the mark. She motioned for Aequus to join her. "Let us help with this, at least."

Atrox watched in silence as they joined their palms and pressed on Darkness' brand. Their power flowed through his arm, and he sensed that odd burning again, followed by a cooling sensation, then it was gone. One glance confirmed the mark had been removed, for good.

The wolf god rolled his shoulder, then met his siblings' gazes. "If I was to come back…what of Catriona?"

The other deities shared a look. "Whatever you wish, brother. Bring her to meet us, whenever you get a chance. We only wish you well."

He nodded, and said, "I'll think on it. For now, I have a quest to finish."

CHAPTER 7

Saluting Ardea and Aequus, the wolf god left them behind and continued to move through what was *not* the underworld. Luckily, his siblings had not added to his list of wounds, but rather healed the mark. It felt freeing not having it over his head any more.

Ainsling fluttered around him. "You're quiet."

Atrox shrugged, his eyes inspecting the surroundings. "Trying to determine how bad the next challenge will be." He paused, then said, "Any news from Catriona?"

The pixie shook her head. "Not since I last saw her."

"How was she?"

"My answer will not change, wolf god. She was waiting for you."

He sighed, ran a hand through his messy hair, and wished like hell he could find a lake to dunk his face in. From the dust to the flames, he was grimy and in dire need of a wash.

As though catching onto his thoughts, the passage he was in opened abruptly onto a cave, and a lake. Its blue iciness, almost white, was odd in the otherwise dour decor of the place.

Atrox paused in his steps. "If this is not the underworld,"

he said, "is it fair to say Merlyddus created it?"

"Mhmm."

"And that frozen lake must be my next challenge?"

Ainsling nodded again, though she seemed perturbed by its appearance. "Watch your step. Who knows how thin the ice is?"

Leaving the pixie behind him, Atrox moved across the surface of the lake, the sword dangling from his hand.

He hadn't realized it this time, but the temperature had changed. Frowning, he stepped once more, and something cracked. His gaze went to the ice underneath him – and the thin line now marring its surface, directly under his foot. "The sword!" Ainsling yelled from above him. "It's weighing you down!"

Atrox looked up to tell the pixie to mind her own business. But the minute his mouth opened, the crack under him got bigger, and then the ice broke.

His body sank like a boulder through the ice-cold water. The sword in his hand dragged him further down, as if possessed by another life.

Atrox tried to fight it, to no avail. He couldn't let go of it anymore, either. His fingers were glued to it. On and on they went, his lungs catching fire as the water around him got icier and icier.

The last thing he remembered was cold....then darkness.

Shivers roused him from sleep. His body temperature was always hot, and the bone-deep iciness in his veins was new.

Atrox blinked against the fog, then stood up and dragged himself in a standing position. *Merlyddus is really enjoying keeping me on my toes.*

He was in some kind of inner cave, no longer in the lake, but out on the shoreline. Despite the chill in the air and his own breath coming out in puffs, the water called to his parched throat and he crawled to it.

How much time did I waste with all this unconsciousness shit?

Each wasted minute was another Merlyddus gained – and he was done letting the fool Fae king win. He cupped some of the water and drank his fill, until his thirst had been quenched.

No matter, Atrox thought. *If it takes me years and eons, I will still reach you, Catriona.*

A swish behind had him reach for his sword – until his eyes fell on the person standing merely a few feet away.

"I.... you...."

Atrox gulped, at a loss of words. It should have been impossible, but somehow he'd known, deep in the darkest corner of his soul, that *she* would be among the challenges.

And she was beautiful, still. Blonde hair in curls to her waist, blue eyes like the colour of the sky, and a mouth he'd kissed many eons ago. She smiled at him, and her name finally escaped his numb lips.

"Deasa."

She had been his lover, the Juliet to his Romeo in the pantheon of gods. They had been envied, worshipped.... And then his rebellion had fallen through, and they had been taken captive.

It must be a dream. Another illusion.

As if guessing his thoughts, Deasa shook her head. "I'm

no dream, Atrox."

"But... you died."

The smile grew regretful. "Can you not admit the truth to yourself, my love? I didn't just die, Atrox. I killed myself."

The memory lingered between them as if it had just happened.

Ignoring his siblings' raging cries, he turned to Deasa and met her gaze. "I will keep you safe."

Her blue eyes met his, and he saw a pure love shining within. Deasa had always been his opposite, gentle where he was hard, loving when he was ruthless. The only one he had ever given his heart to – and ever would for his existence.

It was why Atrox never forgave himself what happened next.

One moment, Deasa leaned her lips towards his, kissing his anger away. Just as he prepared to deepen the kiss, her body jerked unnaturally. Atrox pulled away to see her eyes glazing over, death in their depths.

He looked down, not comprehending what had taken place, even with the evidence presented: a silver blade protruding from her robe.

Unwilling to live in the underworld, Deasa had stabbed herself with the one weapon that could kill her – a dagger Atrox had gifted her, for self-defense. A blade created out of the very crater their pantheon's entrance existed at.

Atrox grasped Deasa in his arms and removed the offending metal. Red blood, the color of dark rubies, flowed out of her body. With one hand, Atrox tried to staunch it, using his powers. But where they should have healed, they did nothing.

Atrox remembered begging for her life, and the pain in his chest at losing her. It was as present in his mind as everything else, but he could not rouse any anger at her for the choice she had made.

Instead, a fresh wave of sorrow shuddered through him. "Why, darling?" He took a step closer. "I would have protected you."

She reached for his cheek. "I know. And we could have been happy...but I did not belong in the underworld."

Atrox let himself sink into her touch. A part of him warned he should be careful, that he should not give in to it, for fear of betraying Catriona. But this was Deasa, and his heart had not been quite right since her death. He'd refused to allow himself to love, to admit that he could still love... Another realization nagged at the back of his mind, but he pushed it aside.

"What do you mean?" He had to know, now, if he never saw her again.

"You were always so strong, Atrox," Deasa said. "Always a leader, a survivor. It was one of the many reasons I fell for you, and loved you with all my being. But when we were in front of your siblings, and they cast their punishment..."

She shuddered, then forced her eyes to open. The light blue singed his heart, and Atrox knew a part of him would always care for her, just as he would always feel her loss. "I could not follow, my love. Not in the underworld, where I would lose the last of my light."

Atrox inhaled sharply, hearing the pain in her voice. A lone tear slid on her cheek, and he reached with his thumb to wipe it away. "I have missed you, my darling."

"And I, you," Deasa whispered.

Cold air drifted over him, and he felt chilled to the bone once more. Realizing time was running away, he shook himself out of the daze and asked the harder question. "Why are you here?"

Deasa stepped closer, her blue eyes filled with love, and peace. "You know why. To bring you to your hardest challenge."

Atrox looked at her, then around. The pixie was nowhere to be seen. "Love, you mean."

She hummed in agreement, then took his hand. Atrox expected her to drag him somewhere in the darkness, but instead he fell into another sleep.

≈ ♠ ≈

Atrox's eyes opened to a throne room. He was in a familiar palace in his pantheon. He remembered being brought here in chains, facing a trio of judges – his siblings, and Vulper. Deasa had been by his side, as had been Faitus.

"Is this your idea of a court of justice?" Atrox spoke, his thunderous voice echoing across the empty surface. His words were followed by a sneer. "Even humans can do better."

"Silence!" The rumbling warning from Aequus only earned him a laugh. "You are not here to speak, lower –"

"Cut through the shite, brother," Atrox taunted, enjoying the sudden quaintness, as though no one dared to breathe. "Let's face it, you and my dear sister want me out. You have ever since you let Vulper into our little trio."

Atrox turned a flaming gaze to the red-haired man, before meeting Ardea's green and black eyes. "You know what I mean."

The tone was accusing, but she refused to rise to the bait. Lifting her chin in a gesture that truly showed their familiar liens, Ardea stated, "You were never pushed out."

The memory left him and he shook his head. On his heels, he turned in a circle, until his eyes fell on a figure in the distance. Blonde hair curled to a small waist, hidden beneath ragged robes. Heart beating faster, he ran to her.

"Deasa!"

Perhaps that was his challenge – to stop her from killing herself.

"Deasa, don't! I can save you, I–"

She turned to him, but it was not blood on her robe, nor did she seem saddened. Her face was glowing with joy. Her blue eyes glittered, and her rosebud mouth was upturned at the corners. And in her arms was a tiny bundle, wrapped in a soft material.

Atrox froze in his steps, but it did not stop Deasa from inching closer to him.

"You already saved me, darling," she whispered as she reached him.

This is a dream.

He tried to warn his mind, but her scent enveloped him, and he stared like a fool at the life blooming in her rosy cheeks. Then his gaze dropped to what she carried. Eyes as dark at his stared back at him, with hair as blonde as hers. Emotion welled up in his eyes, and his throat clogged.

"Deasa…"

"Why do you look so shocked?" Her laugh echoed in the large room, and she rose on tiptoes to kiss his cheek. "Would you hold your son? He's been asking for you all morning."

Before he could say anything, she had already extended the tiny bundle towards him. Atrox had never felt so inadequate – or afraid. Heart pounding, he held out his arms and the baby was placed in them. He fussed for a moment, then nuzzled deeper into his arms and closed his eyes, suckling on his thumb.

Atrox felt like he'd been anchored to the tiny being. Afraid to move, he simply remained standing, frozen in time. Deasa whispered something about being right back, but he was too entranced by the tiny child to respond.

For long moments, all he did was stare. Then he untangled one arm and lifted it towards his face. The baby seemed much too small in comparison with his paw-like hand, and he hesitated to touch him, fearing he might accidentally hurt him.

"He doesn't bite, you know."

Atrox jerked up and looked behind, noticing Deasa gazing on them with a fond smile. His movement, however, had awakened his son, who fussed in his arms. Noticing the index finger near his face, he reached out with chubby hands and pulled it down to his mouth, and started chewing on it in delight.

Deasa chuckled at Atrox's stunned expression, and wrapped her arms around his waist, resting her head on his shoulder. He noticed she was wearing a different robe, in a blue so light it made her eyes stand out even more.

"What is this place?" Atrox asked, tearing his eyes from his son.

"What do you mean?"

He swallowed past the lump in his throat, though his voice was more hoarse than usual when he next spoke. "My challenge... What is it, Deasa? Why show me all this?"

She bit her bottom lip, chewed on it for a bit, before meeting his eyes once more. "Do you have to think of the challenge? Can't you just stay here, with us?"

Atrox froze, and glanced back at his son. At the back of his mind, he knew this was nothing but another illusion. But the baby felt so real in his arms, and Deasa's presence nearby...

I can only choose one. And I made my choice a while ago.

He looked back at Deasa, but she was already reaching for his son. Her eyes smiled sadly. "You love her so much that you would give this up, too?"

Atrox cleared his throat and said, "This and more, Deasa."

She nodded, then reached out and touched his jaw. Darkness covered him anew.

≈ ♠ ≈

By the time he came to, Deasa was standing up from his side, already walking away.

"Wait!" Atrox cried, struggling to stand, and Deasa turned around once more. "Was any of that real?"

She shook her head. "Does it matter? You made your choice, darling."

"I never meant to hurt you," he whispered. "Are you really..."

A sad smile. "I died long ago, my love. But your memory of me existed... pulled forth by a king after his own devices. If I had crossed into our divine ever after, I would have found you."

Like the memory of her death, the possibility of all they could have had filled the air between them. Atrox clenched his fists, trying not to reach out for her – she had gotten through his walls, at a time when he didn't think he had any. She had forced him to care, once upon a time. But he had moved on.

Deasa smiled and lifted on her tiptoes, kissing the corner of his mouth. Their lips brushed, just barely, in the goodbye they'd never had. "Be happy, my love. Your choice is not wrong, nor should you doubt it. Shed everything else, tear it all apart, and go after what you truly desire."

Before he could do anything else, she left, disappearing in the fog. Atrox sank against the cavern walls. His onyx gaze was thoughtful for long, long moments. Then, finally, he picked up his sword, stood on determined legs and marched onwards.

"Seven challenges, Merlyddus said. Which means the exit is near."

And Catriona, even more so. The thought made his pulse turn to molten lava. After all these challenges, they had much to discuss.

If only I could get to her already...

CHAPTER *8*

Rather than the uneven but flat terrain he'd covered so far, Atrox found himself going uphill. His gut told him he'd been underground – even more so than before – and that he was getting back to the surface. It proved to be right, as he caught sight of the rest of the tunnel ahead.

Just as he was about to quicken his speed, something trickled on top of him. He glanced up, surprised to see something akin to rain falling on him. Only, rather than being transparent, the drops were jet-black and hard as diamonds when they dropped all over him.

Atrox ducked his head and lifted his arm to blast a shield of protection. Much like with Vulper, his powers sizzled out, and his jaw tightened. *Damn Merlyddus and his meddling!* It seemed the old king was determined to make every moment of his quest miserable.

Repurposing the arm to cover his head, Atrox pushed forth and quickened his pace. Air was becoming less, choking him and withdrawing all breath. And still the rain dropped on him, battering his body.

He hissed in pain as a raindrop as large as his fist

hammered into the skin of his already scraped back. Blood jutted out of the cut, and the wound slowed him down.

Is this the last of my challenges? Surviving pain? After everything Merlyddus made me go through, it's almost a letdown.

Refusing to back down, he hardened his muscles and kept going. The tunnel was almost within reach now. "If you think this'll stop me–"

Something fell from the sky as big as a boulder, slamming straight into his shoulder. A crack of bone echoed, and Atrox dropped to a knee from the impact. A low groan escaped him, but he clenched his teeth to avoid giving in to the scream forming in his throat.

Instead, he swallowed it back and pushed off the ground with his fist. Though he stumbled and his balance was off, Atrox refused to give up. The stubborn will in him that had always egged him forth would not give in. He growled instead, and lifted a bloodied face to the ceiling.

"You're afraid I'm getting close to her, aren't you? Catriona's just past this next challenge, and I'll be damned if after all the shite you put me through, you get to win. I will get to her, and show her all the ways we belong together."

He inhaled deeply, then shouted, "And you can't do *anything* about it!"

Another boulder dropped out of nowhere, but Atrox sidestepped it this time. Smirking, he ducked his head and emerged back onto the road he'd known so well.

Wobbly on his feet, Atrox dropped to his knees, holding himself up by his fists. Everything in his body was clamoring rest, and healing. Yet after seeing Deasa, all he could think of how much more he needed to get to Catriona.

He had lost love once… And it had been nowhere the extent of the feelings he had for Catriona. Already his steps were carrying him away further inside the cavern, even as his thoughts turned elsewhere.

The image of the baby he'd left in Deasa's arms filled his mind, causing an odd void in his chest. Could he have had that future, had he not been so ambitious? Could everything have been different?

"Why the mood, wolf god?"

Atrox glanced up, startled out of his thoughts. Ainsling was fluttering by his side, and by the looks of it had been for a few moments. Enough, at least, to catch on to his emotions.

His gaze narrowed on the pixie. "Where have you been?"

It shrugged, avoiding his gaze. "Away."

"To Catriona?"

"Perhaps." The pixie grinned with pointy teeth. "Will you tell me now, or do I have to guess?"

Atrox scowled and started walking again. "There is no reason to my mood." The lie tasted like ashes on his tongue.

"Really?" Ainsling's voice held a tone of haughtiness, almost accusation.

"Yeah," Atrox said, and focused on putting one foot in front of the other. Blood still gushed over his back, but he refused to stop and heal it, not when he was so close. Memories of a flowery scent, blue eyes and flaming curls gave him all the strength he needed to move on.

"You should heal your back."

He spared a glare over his shoulder to Ainsling, but did

not slow down his gait. "It can wait."

"Not if you want to get out of here alive." When he didn't answer, she added, "Unless you wish to remain here, with your former flame."

Atrox stopped then and faced the pixie fully. His eyes narrowed. "What are you on about?"

Violet eyes stared at him accusingly, then one word dropped from her lips. "Deasa."

His chest moved in a different rhythm, the gust of rage making his pulse race. "Not that I owe you an explanation, but I didn't ask to see Deasa, nor my so-called child. The whole damn thing was an illusion."

"One you seemed to want to believe very much."

Atrox shook his head. "Unbelievable. I don't have time for this." He turned to leave, but Ainsling fluttered in front of his face again.

"Don't you think Catriona deserves someone who isn't hung up on a former love?"

"I am not hung up on Deasa! Did that challenge not prove it?" Atrox pinched the bridge of his nose, wincing as the movement pulled on his back muscles, and the wound there. "At one time, I loved Deasa. She was the first goddess to really catch my feelings, to awaken something in me. But nothing – *nothing!* – compares to what I feel for Catriona."

He looked up and met the pixie's gaze. "Don't you understand? I loved Deasa, wanted to protect her. But Catriona – she gets to me like no one else. She's the flame pulling me closer, and I don't care how badly I get burned if it means I can be by her side."

Ainsling maintained their eye contact a moment longer,

then nodded. "Be it so, wolf god."

In silence, they took off once more.

After another few hours of walking, Atrox emerged out of the cavern into another large enclosure. This time, he knew he had reached the end of the road. It was hard to miss the exit – a large portal shone in the middle, beckoning him forth.

Which was why Atrox was perplexed.

"What holds you back?"

Atrox glanced at the door again. Eagerness to see Catriona ran through him, but he also hesitated. *This is too easy.*

"You survived seven rather arduous challenges that showed you more than you bargained for about yourself. And now... What, you hesitate?"

Atrox scowled. "Stop implying I'm a coward while you're ahead." Still, his feet kept him rooted to the ground until he finally said, "Six."

"Hmm?"

"It was six challenges to date. Brawn, brains, greed, honesty, family and love." His eyes narrowed. "How do you count seven?"

Ainsling snorted. "Have you ever thought perhaps your first challenge was getting through the portal in the first place? Merlyddus never thought you would take him up on his offer, and allow yourself to be a toy at his command."

Atrox's jaw clenched at the description, but he forced himself to take a deep breath as the pixie continued, unaware of his agitation.

"Or perhaps the rain was the last of it, who can say? Either way, both those instances showcase two ways Merlyddus fully expected you to turn around, but I suppose he did not know you well." Ainsling looked up then, finally noticing his darkening expression, and flew a distance away. "Err, that is to say... Sorry."

"Bit late for that, no?" Atrox said, his voice low and vibrating with anger.

Ainsling glanced at the door, and back at him. "All of Merlyddus' machinations aside, you've made it this far. Why the pause?"

Atrox didn't really know it himself. For the last days he'd been in this fake reality, fighting to get to somewhere so he could get Catriona to forgive him. Yet he still didn't have a speech ready, let alone a compelling argument to explain why they should be together.

Past a dry throat, he managed, "How is she?"

Ainsling was quiet for so long, he feared she would deny him that. In the end, she said, "My mistress awaits you."

"She knows I'm coming?"

"She has kept an eye on you for a long time, wolf god."

He recalled the dreams, and his body tightened in anticipation. *Enough of this weakness,* he scolded himself. Step by step, he forced his feet to move towards the portal.

The closer he got, each step became heavier.

"What is this sorcery?"

The pixie's voice was soft, emotion filling it. "Only one more test."

Atrox tried to turn and glare, but could only move his head. "That blasted king!" Fury raged through his blood, battling against the spell, but it was no use. He was too weakened from the challenges, and at the Fae's mercy. "I thought you said all seven challenges were met!"

Ainsling said nothing for a long moment. Finally, she whispered, "In order to cross, the price is blood – divine or Fae. But whoever's blood you spill, that person becomes mortal for all eternity."

It took a moment for the riddle to sink in.

"You're saying all I have to do is give my blood, and I'll get to Catriona. But in order to do so, I lose my immortality?"

The pixie nodded. As if losing such a piece of him, that he'd fought for so hard in the last years, was easy.

"Or I spill Fae blood.... and I walk out unscathed?"

"Yes."

Atrox clenched his fists. "And where the hell am I supposed to find Fae blood in this dump?'

Ainling flew in front of him, not quite meeting his gaze. In a whisper, she said, "I have enough Fae in me to count."

Atrox stared in shock for a moment, then snorted. "There's *hardly* enough Fae in you to sacrifice."

The pixie squeaked, then said, "True. Which is why you'd have to sacrifice me, fully."

Its hand flew in the air, and a knife materialized. Ainsling fluttered even closer, almost touching his nose, as she handed the knife to him. Atrox took it, his jaw slack.

"One drop of my blood versus your life? What an easy choice."

The pixie bowed its head, as if resigned. But the knife did not cut in.

Instead, Atrox threw his head back and growled. His clenched fists glowed, his powers no longer restrained, and the entire place shook on its foundations. Ainsling flew backwards in alarm.

"What are you doing? You'll bring the whole place down!"

Gritting his teeth, Atrox ignored her. With all his might, his will as a god, his love for Catriona, he fought against Merlyddus' spell. *I refuse to be stopped so close to my goal.*

Sweat beaded on his forehead, and his body tensed under the weight of what he was doing. Still, he didn't give up. Ainsling's pleas fell on deaf ears as Atrox focused all his intention on his surroundings.

Pieces of rock fell from the ceiling, and dust lifted from the ground. Then, like an elastic band pulled too tightly, the spell holding him was demolished and he was able to move.

The first thing he did was throw Ainsling's knife away. "What stupid king is this?"

Shaking his head, Atrox instead walked back to the sword he had tossed away and picked it up. Without a flinch, he cut into his palm, then closed his fist over the blood and walked back to the portal.

This time, he was prepared for the heaviness trying to take its toll on him, and shook it off. "I've done your damned challenges, now let me *through*!" He yelled, and tossed the blood into the portal.

It glowed red for a moment, then went back to a clear light. The heaviness disappeared and Atrox was able to move once more. He kept the sword in his hand this time, refusing to be weakened if Merlyddus awaited him on the other side with his entire Fae entourage.

Ainsling flew in front of him then, staring in disbelief. "I don't understand. Why spare me and lose all you are?"

Atrox looked back at his bleeding hand and snorted.

"What kind of immortal would it make me, if my choice was any different?"

Silence only answered him, and had him glance up once more. He was no longer in the cavern... but in a meadow, with vibrant skies and grass. In the distance was a cliff, overlooking a valley filled with water and more forest. And by that cliff...was Catriona.

CHAPTER 9

His Fae queen startled him, looking drop dead gorgeous in a green wrap dress. Her wings, unlike before, were unbound and fluttering against her back. Her hair was loose, in flaming locks over her creamy shoulders.

In her tingling voice, she said, "It makes you the kind of immortal worthy of me."

Atrox took a step closer, then another. "I don't understand." He felt oddly unworthy of being around her, filled with grime and blood as he was. But nothing could have kept him away, drawn as he was by her.

"Your question, about the kind of immortal you are... Your choice made you worthy of me." Catriona's blue eyes were wary, but she did not try to evade him. "It was I who added the last test. Ainsling was right, and wrong. My father didn't stop at seven challenges. After the first one – for you to cross into the portal, and agree to his terms, thus relinquishing your control – he was not pleased. When he saw you were succeeding, he added another. The last official challenge *was* the rain – hoping the regret of the choice you made, to leave Deasa behind, would weigh you down and you would be unable to escape."

"You…saw everything, then?"

Catriona nodded, her blue eyes searching his. Was it his imagination, or was there a flicker of something responding in those depths?

It took a second for her admission to register. When it did, Atrox had to force down his innate need to destroy – being manipulated, he did not like. Still, he could not avoid a scowl. "So you added a challenge, putting your pixie's life on the line… Why? Your father's seven, eight, however many, were not enough?"

Catriona shook her head. "Always so stubborn."

"Stubborn?" Atrox took a step closer, then forced himself to inhale deeply. "Do you have *any* idea of the hell I've just been through?"

"I know you don't like being challenged. Or put through hoops. This was not–"

Atrox was on her in the next breath, his hand at her nape, pulling her close, desperately trying to hold back, but unable to. His lips meshed against hers with no finesse, no tenderness, just pure passion – and rage against being separated for so long.

To his relief, Catriona wrapped both her arms around him and moaned against his lips, pulling herself closer to him. Almost as if she too, couldn't get enough, despite his mediocre appearance and the blood she was getting all over herself.

After long moments of plundering her mouth, Atrox pulled back just enough to whisper, "That was not the hell I spoke of, Catriona. Being without you, unable to hold you, kiss you, hear these delightful sounds you make…*that* was the worst punishment."

Then he kissed her again, more tenderly this time. A fire was being stoked between them, and he was not sure how much longer he could contain it. There was nothing better than having her in his arms, but he was well aware of his own appearance, and the grime covering him.

Finally, Atrox pulled back, though he kept both arms on her waist. "I don't care what challenge you put me through, my Fae queen. You've but to ask, and I will bring down the moon and the stars for you."

Catriona's eyes shone with unshed tears. "Atrox... You're not angry?"

"Not for that, no," he said truthfully. "But I am angry about how you left me – and having to play your father's games, just to get to you. Was the whole quest your idea, then?"

Catriona shook her head, and a tear escaped her. He kissed it off her cheek, even as she whispered, "My father... After Carleigh penetrated my kingdom, my father appeared. In order to get the last bit of information – of how to get rid of the sorcerer – there was a price to pay."

Atrox stilled then, all breath cut out of him. "He asked you to return here, didn't he? And leave me behind."

Catriona nodded, closing her eyes against the rage she felt coming off him in waves. "You may believe me weak, or cowardly, for not fighting him off. But, Atrox–"

He shut her up with another kiss, though he did not linger. "I think no such thing."

"But–"

Atrox lifted an index finger to her lips, trying to ignore the way their softness stirred him everywhere. *This is important, and I have only one try.*

"You sacrificed your freedom for me – for those I care about. Without you, we never would have been able to defeat Carleigh, nor help Vivienne survive. You…" He shook his head, then dropped his forehead to hers, even as he moved his hands to her shoulders.

Tears ran down her cheeks now freely, and her eyes took on the faintest hue of blue he had ever seen.

"You are everything for me, Catriona, and you did nothing wrong. On the contrary, it is I who owe you an apology."

She sniffed, and frowned. "Whatever for?"

"Had I not been afraid to voice my feelings, I might have been there when your father gave you the ultimatum. I could have fought him for you."

Catriona shook her head. "Not a good idea, he's rather–"

"Powerful?" Atrox smirked. "I know I look like shit, but do you really believe I cannot take him in a fight?"

Catriona leaned further into his embrace, tilting her head back to smile up at him. "Hmm… I suppose you *are* rather stubborn, lover."

Atrox's eyes shone with the confidence of a god. "Is that all I am, Catriona? A lover, and nothing else?"

Her lips parted, ready to give him the answer he wanted, but they were interrupted. From the sky, Fae soldiers dropped on the ground, surrounding them in a circle. Then a flash of lightning opened a portal and Merlyddus stormed out, his expression sour.

"So. You made it through."

Atrox shrugged, and moved so he was in front of

Catriona, shielding her with his body. "I did. And we had a deal."

Merlyddus snorted. "What you wish will not be possible, for the simple reason you will not be around to see it."

Atrox bent his upper body forward, and scowled. "You want to do this again, king? Remember what happened in the realm of dreams?"

Merlyddus smirked. "Ah, but we are not in dreams, wolf god. We are in reality, and I always win."

Atrox clenched his fists, already calling on his divine energy. Before Catriona could do anything, the first Fae moved forward with a spear, and Atrox yanked it out of his hands. He was too focused on the fight, not realizing that his Fae queen was ready to lose it.

"Enough."

The air around them filled with electricity, and everyone paused in their movements. Merlyddus stared in shock. Atrox turned to Catriona – but she was unlike anything he had seen before. She was angry, her blue eyes dark, flashing with lightning. Wind surrounded her, making her flaming locks of hair dance like snakes. She was gorgeous, and it humbled him even more when he realized she was protecting him.

"I am not a child anymore, and too long I have let you dictate my life. You *will* approve of my choice," Catriona said. "I am done fighting you over this, father."

Merlyddus scowled. "You are my blood, pure Fae, descendant of the greatest of our kind. You are not free to make up your mind in this instance."

Catriona dropped her hands, her expression filling with sadness. "Will you really deny me? Not as a worthy descendant to carry your line, but as your daughter?"

The pain filling every word vibrated in the air, and the Fae soldiers shifted restlessly. Plainly, they were as uncomfortable with this display of emotion as Merlyddus was.

The king stared in shock at his daughter, then something came over his features. It was not regret over how he had acted, but resignation at her decision. He dropped his staff away from Atrox. "Is there really no one else to make you happy?"

Catriona took a step by Atrox's side, intertwining their hands together. She smiled up at him. "No one but him."

Out of the corner of his eye, Atrox saw Merlyddus nod, and heard his sigh as he said, "Then so be it."

But he could not have cared less. He would have fought them all – and more – if it meant being with her. His arm snaked around Catriona's waist, pulling her closer to him as he inhaled her scent. Her hand went up his back, tracing the bloody wound, and he sensed her magic healing it.

None of it mattered. Only the feel of her in his arms did.

Then Merlyddus shifted, and it drew his attention. His staff hit the ground once more, but this time a portal erupted, engulfing the two lovers. The next moment, the Fae soldiers had disappeared and they were in a blue paradise.

Inhaling deeply, Atrox looked down at Catriona.

CHAPTER 10

"Where, exactly, are we?" He glanced around at the vivid trees, the lake underneath… It was all much too familiar.

"This cannot be your kingdom. Your real one was destroyed, no?"

Catriona looked around as though in a daze, and left his embrace to take in the full landscape. Her wings disappeared in her back, as they always did when she was resting. Surprise coated her voice when she whispered, "My father must have recreated it."

Atrox could not stand the distance between them. In two swift strides, he was by her side, grabbing her wrist and turning her to him. Their lips met once more, and she gave in to the kiss, pliant and ready for him.

Atrox pulled back then, and smoothed her hair. "Thank you, for standing up to your father for me."

She smiled up at him. "Not that you needed it."

Her hands roamed his bare chest, and he groaned at the touch. "Before we give in, there is something I need to say." But Catriona was already engrossed in his muscles, her light fingertips tracing them. It was with regret he grabbed her hands, stopping their exploration, in order to gain her attention.

"I am sorry, my darling." He let go of one hand to cup her cheek in his. "The pain I put you through, you did not deserve it. I should have said these words when you left, I should have done… a lot more. I am sorry, from the bottom of my heart."

He let go of her then, and slipped to one knee in front of her. "If you'll allow me, I will spend the rest of this immortality making it up to you."

When only silence answered him, he looked up to see she was covering her mouth, trying to smother her sobs. He straightened and gathered her close, relishing once more the feel of her in his arms.

After she'd cried on him for long moments, Catriona whispered, "You are forgiven." Then she pulled back, and held his hand. "Come with me."

For a few moments they walked in silence, then emerged by the side of a lake. Like he'd done in the past, Atrox shed his clothes and followed her inside the crystalline water, which did nothing to hide Catriona's curves.

Ducking under the water, he felt its cleansing properties, the wound in his back completely closing. When he broke the surface once more, his hair was plastered to his scalp, and water dripped in rivulets over his chest.

Catriona watched him from afar, her blue eyes glowing, a soft smile on her lips.

After a few strokes in the water, he could not hold it back anymore. He reached for Catriona, and she came to him like a dream, wrapping her legs around him. Atrox groaned in her neck, feeling her heat so close to him.

His hand moved from her waist to her breast, toying with a nipple. His mouth found hers, and he groaned in the kiss.

Before he could control the lust spreading in them, Catriona opened for him and pulled him inside her. He groaned again at the heat of her, the tightness, even as she whispered in his ear.

"More, Atrox… My wolf god."

He grabbed her waist with both hands and thrust inside of her, until her pleasured scream echoed to the empty sky, and she curled around him like a satisfied cat.

Atrox moved through the water, and laid them both on the warm rocks. He was playing with her hair when Catriona said, "I also have something to apologize for – your challenges. My father made you go through a lot of painful memories, in order to prove your worth to me."

He shrugged. "Not all were bad, my love."

In detail, he explained what they had been. Deasa's was the hardest to get through, and his voice became hoarse with emotion. Catriona held his hand through it all, then he spoke.

"Merlin and Morgana…."

"I'm sure my brother has figured out life by now," Catriona smiled. "Which means we are free to focus on us. Unless Vivienne…"

Atrox smiled and pointed to the water. "She is well with Sébastien…. Though they made me promise to visit."

"That can be arranged," Catriona smiled.

She nuzzled closer, kissing his neck, and his entire body answered the unspoken invitation. His hand moved to her waist, and Catriona chuckled against him. "Again?"

He nibbled on her shoulder, then tugged her atop him

and slid inside her. Her soft mewls were music to his ears, and he enjoyed the darkening of her eyes in desire. "For all eternity, my love."

The moon rose above them, witness to their love. It had been a long time coming, but even the wolf god had been able to find his soul mate. And for that alone, the stars themselves had to bear witness.

The End

If you liked The Avalon Chronicles,
try one of my other series!

For a sneak peek at my urban fantasy
(young adult) series,
check out The Sage's Legacy!

If you're in the mood for a different type
of paranormal romance, the Moonlight
Rogues
are waiting for you ☺

Or there's always my standalone
novels!

Preview of First to Fall
(Moonlight Rogues, Book 1)

∞ 1 – Începuturi ∞
"The beginning is the most important part of the work."
-Plato-

Lucrezia

My feet crunch in the snow, and for the tenth time this morning I thank my lucky stars I invested in my fuzzy warm boots. It may have been money I didn't have, but with the way the winter is acting up, it will only get worse.

Rockland Creek, Wyoming, is renowned for its harsh winters—not that it's the real reason I ended up here. It was the most remote place near the border with Canada and having that quick escape possible eases the tightness in my back somewhat.

Memories of a much darker time linger at the edge of my consciousness, but I shake them off. Distance and months of breathing freely have made it easier to compartmentalize, and I'm determined to get in to work chipper despite the chilly Monday morning.

An icy gust of wind sweeps up, and I huddle in my coat, wishing I had grabbed an extra sweater underneath it.

Almost there. As if to spite me, Mother Nature throws in some nice flurries—and more wind. Gritting my teeth against it, I quicken my step towards Claws Auto Shop, which I see in the distance. I'm one of those lucky few who can walk to work rather than have to drive or bus, which keeps me in an overall nice shape and clears my mind most mornings.

Most times, it only takes me about half an hour to get there. It's a breeze in summer, but not so much in winter. I vaguely consider asking one of my colleagues for a lift for the rest of the season and then dismiss the idea. The last thing I want them to feel is obligated to protect the only girl in their pack.

By the time I finally reach the side door of Claws Auto Shop, where I work as receptionist, my cheeks are frozen and my fingers refuse to cooperate. I fumble with the key, dropping it three times in the snow, before I get the blasted thing open.

After taking off my coat and switching into some comfortable sneakers, I sit down at my small desk and get started on my day. Within the next hour, as I answer calls and confirm appointments, the guys pile in one by one.

Guys, no. These are *men* and so damn gorgeous my heart hurts every time I notice them. Unfortunately, other body parts I've neglected for a while also poke their head out. Normally, I have a tight control on my hormones. These last few weeks, however…

I tear my eyes away from them and focus on my paperwork, going through the previous week's sales and amounts for collection. Having studied accounting and business while in university, numbers always fascinated me. They make sense, more so than people ever do—to me, at least. But this time around, not even the dry accounts payable booklet is enough to keep me focused. With every ring of the bell announcing someone's presence, I glance up.

First Finn McConnell shows up, his mischievous green eyes twinkling already. With his mop of unruly dark hair and the lithe body of an athlete, he could easily be an actor or model. The lilt in his voice hints at his Irish background, and yeah it's sexy as hell. You would never peg him for a lawyer, but he once dabbled in the trade before leaving Ireland for the States—a long, long time ago like he says.

Next comes Tristan Cayne, brooding about another sleepless night, if the circles under his eyes are any indication. He's a war vet, honorably discharged from the Marines with PTSD—post-traumatic stress disorder. He lost his entire unit in an ambush in the desert and still has the nightmares about it. His skin is tanned even in winter, due to his Brazilian blood, but the man knows how to pull off jeans and a simple shirt like no other. With his shaved head, gentle hazel gaze and square jaw, he's the most aloof of the four.

Third in is Dominic Kosta, with blue eyes that capture me every time and the sinful body of Apollo. Dark blonde hair, clean-cut jaw and muscular build, he's the gentlest of the bunch. At first he told me he was born and bred here, but after many late evening conversations, he revealed he was adopted from a Romanian orphanage by an American couple who couldn't have children of their own.

The story answered a lot of questions about him, and it gave me more insight into this gentle giant who I've seen break more than one heart with all his womanizing. Despite it, there's a quiet confidence in him I respond to, and he puts me at ease in a way no other man has. I've been working here for the last year, but it's Dominic I connected with more than all the others.

His grin lights his face when he sees me, and he moves in for a hug. I squeal out of his grip, shivering at the wind drafting in with him. "Get away, you're ice cold!"

Dom picks me up snorting and twirls me around, before putting me back down. I'm still recovering from the closeness, when the last of them walks in.

"Already wasting time, I see?" Lucas Bianchi's remark

would have stung, had it not been delivered with his side-smirk and glittering onyx eyes. The man is Italian to the bone, and his commanding presence tends to leave me shaking at the knees.

Lately, it's morphed into more than that. Whenever he's around, I lose my words—and I haven't crushed on anyone since high school.

"Morning, Lucrezia," he murmurs in his gravelly voice, and I smile feebly in return. To this day, Lucas is the only one who calls me by my full name, all the others having picked up on the nickname Dom gave me: Luz, for light.

As can be guessed, the mixed nationalities have definitely increased my vocab, at least where swearing is concerned. Both Tristan and Lucas lose it in their respective native tongues, and it's almost fun watching them when it happens.

With a nod to Dominic, Lucas heads to the back, already barking orders to Finn and Tristan. Two other guys help around the store in summer, but they're only teenagers from high school, learning the trade. Mostly, it's just us five: me on the paperwork and phones, and the guys tinkering and fixing the cars of Rockland Creek—and of the people passing through.

And I was the lucky one who got to work with them every week, day in and day out.

"Why the long sigh?"

Oops. I'm uncannily aware of Dom's steady gaze on me—and his keen sense of observation.

"Bah, it's Monday," I try to joke, but even I don't fall for it. I peek towards Lucas, who's now opening the doors of the garage—a tell-tale sign announcing they're ready for work.

The inside of their working environment has heat

blasting so even with the cool air wafting in, they're comfortable. Not that it seems to matter to these four—they're so hot-blooded a hug from them will have you sweating in no time!

Thankfully for me, a transparent window and well-insulated door separates me from the garage area, and I get to stay indoors and enjoy the warmth.

My gaze is drawn to the two cars already driving in, one of which is a sporty red Mustang convertible. The other is a pickup truck that has seen better days. It's no surprise when Lucas walks over to the Mustang, with Tristan heading to the other car to greet the clients.

"Who the hell drives a car like that in winter?" My eyes narrow in annoyance.

The answer soon makes itself known. A leggy brunette steps out of the car, dressed in dark leggings, thigh-high boots with six-inch stilettos and a white fur coat. Even from afar, I notice her makeup is done to perfection.

Though I'm confident in my flaming locks and exotic features, I don't tend to flaunt my looks. Working with the guys gives me the perfect excuse for casual dress and flying under the radar in jeans and t-shirts.

It's better this way, the reasonable voice in my mind warns. *Remember what happened last time?*

A snort from Dom has me focus back on him, in time to see his grimace.

"What?"

"The girl," he rolls his eyes. "She'll be a handful. I better go, Lucas might need help."

I watch him go, trying to stifle an exasperated sigh—and

failing. "You sure it's not *her* you want to get a closer look at?"

Dom turns around at that, a flash of surprise crossing his features. It's gone so quick I might have imagined it. He grins instead and winks. "Not with you around, Luz."

He's gone before I can figure out what he means, and I turn my attention to my regular tasks. At least until the brunette comes for payment. "I was told to come here to pay for the services," she says huskily, and I wonder for a second if she fakes that voice.

I force a polite smile, realizing how mean my thoughts are turning. "Of course. May I see their quote?" She hands me the paper—perfectly manicured nails, I notice—and I plug it into the computer and issue her a formal invoice.

Once she pays I staple a receipt to the invoice and hand it back to her. Eliza Porting is her name, and if it didn't fit her so classically I would laugh about it. She sounds so posh, dresses to a T, yet here she is in the middle of nowhere with a car that broke down.

You once ended up here in a similar way... I try to ignore the reasonable voice nagging me. A lecture would be bad right about now.

Oddly put off, I hand Eliza back the card and return to my computer. I figure this will be it and she'll go wait in the seating area, but she sees fit to hang around.

"How do you work with all that man candy around?" An annoying giggle follows her whispered words.

I track her gaze to the guys, for a moment detracted when Lucas bends down to check under the car, giving us both a perfect view of his, err, assets. Eliza's practically panting in delight, eyes glued to him solely now.

Mine, I want to growl, and hold back. This possessive nature is new for me, as is the jealousy. I have no right, but Lucas is that kind of man. The type you want to lock up and have your way with, day and night... *especially* night.

"Not sure what you mean," I mutter, focusing on papers that need no more organizing.

She turns to peer at me then—really looks at me, assessing me from head to toe—and smirks knowingly. "Oh, I get it. It's ok; I have nothing against people who play for the other team."

The diva goes back to ogling the guys lasciviously, dismissing me in the process. "More for me."

My palm itches, consumed by an almost insane urge to slap her. Just because I dress a certain way, she needs to label me already? *Bitch.*

I'm about to comment, when her next words hit me hard. "So, seen Tommy lately?" Her lips turn upwards into a sneer at my shocked expression, but those eyes are emotionless.

Shit. I thought I escaped this.

Dominic

I stare at Luz for who knows how long this particular time. At first, I tried to keep my distance. She was new, different, and mortal. But something in her calls to me as sure as the full moon, and the more I've known her these last months, the more I want her.

Unfortunately, she only has eyes for Lucas. She doesn't understand the reason for her attraction is linked to his status as chieftain of our pack. Nor that he officially took the lead as alpha in the summer, causing a hell of a lot of hormonal changes in his scent over the last weeks that affect even the most hardened females.

Then again, Luz also has no idea she's living and working in the midst of a town ruled by werewolves.

Some secret, huh?

We've kept it on the down low from the uninitiated—basically, people like Luz who think the world is normal. Her working for us was a complication at first. We were so used to joking around and acting like mutts in heat that needing to censor ourselves seemed like chaining.

It would have built resentment, were it not for Luz's open perspective on life. She quickly—and bossily—got us all in check, ordering us to treat her like one of the guys. It established a certain professional relationship.

Which is why I'm loath to break it. That, and there was something wounded about her when she first appeared in town. I still remember the day she got off the bus with nothing but a backpack, looking lost and so damn vulnerable it tore at my heart. I was in wolf form, and her scent acted like an aphrodisiac I had a hard time letting go of.

Not many humans are supposed to affect us this way. Not many *do*.

Except Luz.

Back then, despite morphing into my human form, I'd still struggled to quiet my wolf down. I can recall, even to this day, the anxiety in her expression when I first asked if she was new to town. After a few moments of awkward talk, I offered to show her around.

It might have been the loneliness or her quick assessment of me, but Luz agreed. Within the day, we ended up at a diner. No matter how much I tried to probe back then—and since then—the only information I got was that she recently moved to Rockland Creek and was searching for a job.

Before I thought things through, I was already telling her our mechanic's shop direly needed a receptionist. Lucas had been none too happy when I showed up with her in tow, but after some discussion, he relented. Luz was hired the next day, and Lucas has admitted on more than one occasion since that it was the best decision he ever made.

My thoughts of Luz must have intruded on my senses because my wolf is growling. *Danger.*

And no, I don't make a habit of hearing voices, at least not in the losing-my-mind way. But I do have a second facet to my personality, and that's my wolf.

He lives within me, like a subconscious part of me, not an alter ego but more… a voice of reasoning. On a regular basis, he pokes his head out only when strong emotions control me, luring me away from my more human side.

But this time…

I listen to the warning and look towards the reception desk where Luz's anger reverberates across the distance. The high-maintenance gal who's with her irks me, and she annoys my wolf.

"Don't," Finn mutters next to me.

I glance at my buddy, surprised he read me so easily. Then again, with Finn, you're an open book more often than not. That's the thing when you're around werewolves with special *gifts*, like I call them.

"You know she has feelings for Lucas." His eyes narrow in disapproval, darting from Luz back to me.

"And you know *why* she has them," I retort, going back to what I'm supposed to be doing— hammering back into shape a beat-up bumper.

Finn follows me to the long table meant for the task, not dropping the conversation. "You're assuming," he accuses, and I hammer the metal a little too hard.

My back muscles tense, and my wolf jumps to defense when I turn to him. "Back off, Finn."

He notices my glare, because after a few tense moments of staring at each other he steps away, hands held up in the air. "I'm only saying, mate. Keep in mind, Luz may have real feelings and more than a crush on our boss."

I don't believe that. *Won't* believe it, is more like it. And as I sense Luz's annoyance go up a notch, my wolf whines. *We can't sit by and do nothing.*

"Need a coffee." My mutter is barely audible, but I don't wait for an answer, instead storming toward the doors. I step through, and the gal from the city moves towards me like a cat pouncing on her favorite toy. Her overwhelming perfume makes me cough and I take a step sideways.

"Aw, poor baby's got a cold?"

I don't know what my face conveys at her idiotic question, but she backs away so fast she almost trips over her heels. "No, just allergic to perfumes, *miss*." I stress the term for professionalism's sake, before dismissing her and turning to Luz.

Luz's eyes flash towards the client and the scent of anger hits me again, something I seldom see in her. It makes the gold stand out against the green of her eyes, and the image of a cat superimposes itself for a moment in my imagination.

Cats and dogs don't mix, my wolf points out. I stifle a smile at that, and Luz stops glaring at the fake Barbie long enough to spare me a concerned look. "You ok, Dom?"

I fake cough this time and force a sheepish grin. "On second thought, I may be coming down with something. Want to make me one of your special teas?"

Whenever any of us is sick, we go to Luz. She has an insane knowledge of herbal teas and their best properties, which comes in handy. My eyes roam over her as she moves from behind the desk, noticing the jeans and long-sleeved purple top she's wearing. She's shorter than me by a head at least, but damn those curves have my mind wandering in a not-so-innocent way, one too many times a day.

Then Luz grins at my words, and it's quick and bright like the sun appearing after a morning of clouds. I swallow past everything else I want to add—this is not the time. Instead, I pout in supplication, hoping the ruse will work.

Luz glances over at the client, undecided and unwilling to slack on the job. "I'll watch her." My promise comes in a mutter, as I'm none too pleased about spending alone time with the snotty client.

After a moment, Luz bites her lip, but relents and moves to the back. "Her name's Eliza."

I'm staring in confusion after her. Why would she give me the useless piece of information? It's not like I'm planning to ask this girl out. Still, once Luz disappears around the corner, I turn to Eliza. "I'm not sure where you think you've landed, miss, but I would loathe rejecting your business because you're upsetting our staff."

She gapes, evidently used to getting her way. *Spoiled,*

my wolf snorts, and I can't help but agree when she yells, "Upset your staff? How dare you!?"

The urge to roll my eyes is strong, but I hold back—barely. "In case you haven't noticed, we're a quiet town here. Tight-knit group of people. We notice when someone upsets one of us."

Eliza continues to scowl, but now there's a stubborn lift to her chin as if she's thinking of disputing my words. "Not my fault your girl can't take a joke."

A growl slips past my clenched teeth then, and she widens her eyes.

"Leave. Now."

"You can't do that, I already paid!"

"There is such a thing as a refund," I drawl, crossing my arms over my chest.

"I didn't even *do* anything!" She stomps her foot at that—I wish I was joking, trust me.

"Either you keep your mouth shut around Luz, or I kick you out." When I move towards her, she gives up and sits on the far couch. "Thank you. Now stay there until your car is ready."

I turn away, ignoring her glare, and follow Luz to the kitchen, determined to make sure she's ok.

Lucrezia

Dom's a sweetheart, and his actions warm my heart. Even if he offered to stick around so he could chat up little Miss Princess.

I'm aggravated with myself for caring, and even more so for not being able to let it go. Dom fools around, I know this.

He's not a player per se, but he dates enough. In a small town like ours, he's known as a catch—in bed. But never for good.

Enough.

I go about making the honey and cinnamon mixture in the small kitchenette, adding some of the ginger root I keep in the fridge here. Once it steeps enough, I pour it all in a cup and am about to return to the reception area.

I almost smack into Dom, who apparently snuck up behind me and was watching me work.

"Easy," he cups my hands, grabbing the mug from them before it spills and burns me everywhere.

After placing it on the side cabinet, he turns his attention back to me. "You ok?"

I want to answer him, really I do. But I'm struck dumb by his proximity, now in my internal bubble, as I call it. Have I never been this close to him? Or have I only been blind to his charm until today? And why in the hell does it feel like I'm left staring at a real-life Apollo, instead of my best friend?

The broadness of his back seems to dwarf me, and every nerve in my body is aware of our secluded presence. *He could do anything...* My brain tries to backtrack, memories pushing forth, and I half-expect a panic attack.

Yet nothing happens, and that scares me more than the opposite. Either I've lost my mind, or there is something about Dom that makes me feel safe. *Maybe it's because I've known him for so long.*

If I was to reach out, I could touch the muscles of his chest. Even from where I am, heat radiates off him, and something in my stomach unfurls in response.

My breath turns shaky, and this time I can't tell if it's a

panic attack, or emotions…or something else.

"Luz, you ok?"

I glance up at his worried tone and manage a nod that's too stiff. "Yeah, fine. Just…out of breath. Sorry."

He frowns then, those beautiful blue eyes warm and scanning me up and down. My skin tingles, and I take a minute to realize he's holding my elbow, as though afraid I'll topple over.

"You sure?"

"Mhm," is my only intelligent answer. Then, like a coward, I side-step him. "Your tea is getting cold," I mutter over my shoulder, and take off the minute he releases his grip.

Dominic

After the morning incident, the day goes by fairly smooth. Eliza leaves with her damn Mustang, and we get no more high class maintenance clients, only our regular clientele. Finn keeps his mouth shut, and I stay busy with as many things as I can take.

Despite my best efforts, I can't stop watching Luz. I see her blush when Lucas asks her out to lunch to go over the sales reports—which they end up doing on the couch in the reception area. I can smell the waves of arousal off her and want to rip his throat out.

Finn steps in at that point, not fooled in the least by my resenting silence. "He's our alpha, Dom."

I ignore how in my face he is, trying to keep my tone curt as I continue to fiddle with the timing belt. "I'm well aware."

"We promised him loyalty."

I throw the piece on the table, ignoring the clank of metal on metal that echoes. I face Finn, failing to appear calm. "He's still new as alpha. And if I recall correctly, I promised him my obedience as his beta, but not my allegiance—and not forever."

Finn glances towards Luz and Lucas, then back at me. "Pack law is clear, mate."

"He hasn't made a claim." The words are more than a growl, but enough to quiet even my wolf.

Then Lucas gets up to go in his office, and Luz watches him with longing. A thought strikes me and before I have time to reason it through, I'm already moving.

This is a terrible idea.

Or so I keep telling myself, even as my feet inch towards Luz. Before I know it, my mouth is running off again—without me. "I can help."

Luz turns those otherworldly eyes to me, the gold more clear up close, and I gulp. I've never had an issue with women, but hell, this one will be the death of me.

"Dom?"

I snap back to with a very unintelligent, "Huh?"

Luz laughs, and I rub the back of my neck.

"Help me with what?" Again, her eyes slide to where Lucas disappeared to.

"With him."

She turns so fast I'm afraid she got whiplash. "What are you talking about?"

"I can help you with Lucas." I drop on the couch, ignoring her stunned expression and those lips I want to kiss so bad my mouth tingles. "You like him, right?"

Her face falls as she whispers, "Am I that obvious?"

"Only to me," I answer truthfully. "But you *do* like him?"

She nods, her eyes big pools of uncertainty.

"Let me help. I know Lucas, we've been buds forever. If he has feelings for you, he may let rules get in the way. Guy always had a thing for not breaking them."

"What rules?"

I want to smack myself—the reference to our werewolf life slipped too quickly. "Dating work colleagues." I save face and change the subject before she inquires further. "Either way, nothing like dating someone to get him to make a move if he's interested."

"I'm not good at dating," she whispers, looking away.

My wolf points its head, sniffing her scent, which changed in a few seconds. *Fear.* I sense it, too. But of what? Surely it can't be me. Either way, this is a chance to find out more.

"It won't really be dating. We'll fake it for his benefit. If it makes you more comfortable, we can even put a time limit on it. A week, two weeks, whatever you want."

She glances back again towards Lucas as he steps out of his office and back into the garage. The longing in her expression crushes my heart, but I promise myself to rein it in.

"And what's in it for you?" Her gaze is wary when it meets mine.

I shrug. "A chance to annoy him." *And make you happy. And show you he's not the one for you.* That last part, I don't say out loud.

Luz is silent for so long, I'm sure she'll end up saying

no. Besides, what am I thinking? Nothing except selfish thoughts. I want her first kiss, and I want her to at least have the memory of my lips imprinted in her mind before she ends up with Lucas. I want to stake my claim even if it won't be permanent.

"Ok," she surprises me by saying. "How will this work?"

I'm too stunned for a moment to react, but already my wolf is roaring in victory and a grin spreads on my face. "Leave it to me. Meet me tonight for drinks at The Cave, eight o'clock sharp."

When she nods, I lean forward and kiss her cheek, not even surprised when she jumps at the contact. "It'll be fun, you'll see."

And no kidding, I walk away whistling. Yup, like a poor sap who won the girl—not the one who promised to help her get the man of her dreams.

Bite me.

Continue reading!
www.alexawhitewolf.com/books

ABOUT THE AUTHOR

Alexa Whitewolf was born in Romania a little after the fall of Communism, 1992 to be exact. Growing up in the Transylvania region surrounded by epic mountains and a never ending stream of legends and stories was bound to create an overactive imagination. From a young age, she started rescuing pets–abandoned dogs in warehouses, kittens about to be drowned–and spent her childhood talking to animals. This devotion to the furry creatures shows up in her writing, as most of her series will have one–or more–pets involved (think Alistair if you read *The Avalon Chronicles*, Tyr in *The Sage's Legacy*).

The move to Canada in her teens was a sometimes rough adjustment, and Alexa overcame it by burying herself in books–both reading and writing. She started her young adult series at that time, and continued with the fantasy of Avalon in university. Nowadays? She's working on a few other upcoming series, among which a werewolf paranormal romance.

Alexa currently lives nearby picturesque Ontario, where Starbucks locations abound. When not at home writing–or awake in the middle of the night trying to put her characters to sleep–Alexa can be found enjoying walks with her husband and two masters of mischief, Zeus and Achilles. Her social media feed is always inundated with animal posts, so if you're looking for some sunshine in your day, you know where to find it: Facebook, Twitter or Goodreads, so don't be shy!

When the mood strikes, Alexa also dabbles in handmade jewelry and stationery for special occasions, as well as the occasional website creation for friends. And if that's not enough to keep this night owl busy, she's still trying to convince her husband to get another puppy–sadly, a work in progress.

You can read more on her books, enter giveaways and follow her blog on travel, dogs and life in general at www.alexawhitewolf.com

Be sure to sign up for Alexa's mailing list for exclusive perks!

ALSO BY THE AUTHOR

<u>The Avalon Chronicles series</u>
Avalon Dreams
Avalon Wishes
Avalon Nightmares
Atrox – An Avalon Chronicles Novella

<u>The Sage's Legacy – YA series</u>
The Dragon Medallion
The Dragon Manuscript
Relics of the Underworld

<u>Moonlight Rogues series</u>
First to Fall
Second to Surrender
Third to Tumble
Last to Love
Moonlight Rogues: Origins

<u>Standalone novels</u>
Blood Ties, Love Binds
Unconditional Love
Blazing in a Storm of Ashes (Coming Soon)
More novels coming soon!

Sign up for my readers' group **at
www.alexawhitewolf.com/contact** and
receive a copy of *Unconditional Love* for **FREE,**
as well as first dibs on cover reveals,
discounts, giveaways, prizes **and more**!

www.ingramcontent.com/pod-product-compliance
Lightning Source LLC
Chambersburg PA
CBHW021115130626
46554CB00002B/701